Brother's

Keeper

A Novel of Murder and Deception

By
R.W.K. Clark

Edition 1

United States Copyright Office
TX8-286-924 June 2016
Library of Congress Control Number: 2017907157
International Standard Book Numbers
ISBN-13: 978-1948312134 (Paperback)
ISBN-13: 978-0692744741 (Paperback)
ISBN-13: 978-1948312141 (Hardback)
ASIN: B01HBC88UI (Kindle)

/180319

ACKNOWLEDGMENTS

I dedicate this novel to my wonderful readers and for all the amazing people I've met and those I haven't. To my family and loved ones, all your support will not be forgotten.

Thank you

CHAPTER 1

Carly Reed squinted through the darkness at the road before her. She was leaning as close to the windshield of her Beetle as she could, her chin practically resting on her hands as they gripped the steering wheel. She hated driving at night, but she had lost time when she visited Aunt Belle earlier that day, and she couldn't afford to lose more by pulling off the road until dawn. Her big job interview was at ten-thirty the following morning, and if her calculations were correct, she was going to have to drive through the entire night just to get there on time.

The road was deserted except for her, and there were very few lights along the two-lane highway. She looked down at the gauges on her dashboard: a quarter tank of gas left. It should get her to the next town, whatever it was called. She would gas up there for the last time, she decided.

Carly's eyes felt like they were getting heavy. Of course, they were; she had been driving all day, and it was just after one in the morning now. She probably shouldn't be pushing it, but she figured she could load up on coffee in the next town as well. It would be time to fill the tank of the car as well as her own belly.

She reached for the knob on the radio without looking away from the road. In seconds, the car was filled with the sound of pop music. Helping her to wake up just a bit. How far away was the next town, anyway? It seemed to be taking forever.

As if on cue, her headlights picked up the green and white highway sign just a short distance from her. She focused her eyes on the words across the sign:

Burdensville: 10 miles.

"Whew," Carly breathed aloud. "It's about damn time." She had more than enough gasoline to make it ten more miles.

She had just begun to relax when a loud 'crack!' filled the air. Immediately, the Beetle began to fight against her control. She gripped the steering wheel as it jerked from the right to the left, the tiny car began to careen sideways. It took all the muscles she had in her little body to maintain control of the vehicle.

Suddenly, the car came to a stop. It was partially in the road, with its back end on the shoulder in the gravel. Carly's heart was pounding and her breath was erratic. What the heck was that all about?

She shook it off and looked up and down the highway. She saw no headlights coming from either direction. The only light on this stretch was coming from the Beetle's headlights. She was going to have to get out and see what happened.

Carly reached into the tiny backseat and grabbed her industrial-sized Mag-light. She then opened the car door before turning the head on the flashlight to turn it on. Its brightness filled the car and illuminated the ground next to it. She slowly stepped out of the Beetle, continuing to cautiously look up and down the highway for approaching vehicles.

She shined the light on the front driver's side tire, then the rear. Next, she walked to the passenger side. Sure enough, the rear tire was blown, but the word 'shredded' was more appropriate. Damn, she hated dealing with things like this, especially in the middle of the night in a strange place.

She walked back to the driver's side and leaned into the car to turn off the engine and get the keys. Soon, she was staring into the hatch at her spare. The damn thing was just as flat as the one that had blown.

"Damn it!" She stomped her foot on the ground and threw her head back. She felt the tears of frustration coming. It wasn't going to do any good to start crying now, so she struggled to get her wits about her so she could deal with the problem at hand constructively.

Carly shut the hatch and fetched her duffle bag out of the Beetle's back seat. She was going to have to start walking. After locking the car doors, she pulled her smart phone out of her pocket. She would call Road side service and have it towed to Burdensville, where she could have the flat fixed and get back on the road as soon as possible.

But the cell was getting no signal, none whatsoever. After shaking her head in disgust, she put the phone back in her pocket. She would have to deal with it when she got there. Carly began to walk up the highway, her duffle bag slung over her shoulder.

She shined the flashlight in front of her. Her mind was racing as she thought about the interview in the morning. It was her first since graduating college. The position was to teach second grade, and she was so excited that she was beside herself. The thought of missing this interview over a flat tire made her nauseous. She peeled her ears and listened to the sounds around her; there were none. Not even a random coyote or anything. It felt quite… dead.

Carly walked for the next half-hour and even began to hum to herself to take her mind off her problems. She had given up the hope that anyone was going to drive by her; after all, it was just after two now.

No sooner had she pushed that thought from her mind than she heard the rumbling of a car that was missing its muffler. She looked over her shoulder; sure enough a vehicle was coming. It was either a motorcycle or a car with one headlight. In the darkness she couldn't be sure.

She stopped and turned around, letting her flashlight shine in the direction the vehicle was coming from. Then Carly felt her hip pocket; yes, her pocket knife was there. She breathed a sigh of relief that she carried one.

The vehicle was closer now, and it was definitely a car. She began to wave her hands over her head as it neared, and soon the loud old beast was slowing and pulling up beside her.

There was a man behind the wheel, and he leaned over to roll the passenger side window down to talk to her after he turned on the dome light in his car. "Are you broke down?"

"Yes!" Carly replied eagerly. "You can't believe how happy I am to see you."

She silently took note of his appearance. He had thinning hair that could only be described as dishwater blonde, and he wore wire rim glasses. If she had to guess, she would say he was harmless.

"Well," the man said, "I'm going into Burdensville. I can take you there, but there ain't nothin' gonna be open this time of night." He coughed into his fist and cleared his throat. "There is a roadside inn just out of town, though. You could hole up there 'til mornin'."

Damn it! Carly thought. She was going to be forced to reschedule this interview, and she hated to have to do things like that. She shook her head in frustration. "Do you mind if I ride into Burdensville with you?"

"Absolutely!" The man's voice was slurring a bit, but she hardly noticed. She was just so relieved that anyone came to her rescue at all. She was not going to complain.

He reached over and popped the lock on the passenger door, and in seconds, Carly was in the front seat. She put the flashlight and duffle bag on the floor at her feet and then buckled her seatbelt. "Thanks again, mister. You are a real life saver."

"No problem," he said, smiling a friendly smile at her. With that he turned off the dome light and they were soon driving up the dark two-lane highway once more.

The man cleared his throat again. "So, what-cha doin' out here alone, ayuh?"

Carly let out a sigh. "I have a job interview in the morning. I was just trying to make good time."

They drove in silence for a while. Carly was busy lining up her priorities in her head. She wouldn't have the luxury of time from here on out. She needed to be ready to take action first thing in the morning.

"If you want, you could stay on the sofa at my house," the man was saying.

She snapped back to reality. "I'm sorry, I didn't mean to ignore you. What was that again?"

Now his voice took on a tone of frustration. "I said, you can stay on my sofa if you like." Yes, she thought, there is definitely an edge to his voice.

"Thank you, but I think I'll just get a room if it's all the same. I appreciate the offer though."

Silence again. Carly took notice of the next highway sign.

Burdensville 2 miles

No sooner had they passed the sign than the man began to slow down the old vehicle. He took a right onto a narrow gravel road.

"Isn't the town straight ahead?" Carly asked as her heart began to pound.

He glanced at her out of the corner of his eye. "I'm just taking a short cut to take you to the motel."

Suddenly, the driver swung his right arm out violently at Carly, his hand giving her throat what could only be described as a karate chop. Carly grabbed at her throat and struggled to take in air, but all she could get was a gurgle. She began to claw at the seat belt, struggling to breathe. She then grabbed the handle to the door and pulled it, causing the car door to swing violently open, then she flung herself from the vehicle.

Carly hit the gravel hard, her body skidding. The rocks tore the flesh on her face and right arm, and she saw stars as she squawked for breath. She began to pull herself along the gravel.

She could hear nothing, and the thought of the car coming back had not entered her mind. She was in shock, and all she could think about was getting back to the road. Suddenly, there were footsteps in the gravel, and they were coming toward her. She tried to pick up the pace, but she was hurt worse than she knew.

"Now, why didja have to go and do that?" She heard the man's voice clearly; he was right beside her. "Oh, well. It does make things easier on me, so I s'pose I owe you a thankee."

He reached down and grabbed her by her shirt, right behind her head. He violently threw her onto her back

7

and then stood to unbutton his pants. "I s'pose this spot is good as any, girlie."

The man was on her then. She couldn't fight him off; she could barely breathe. He was inside of her then, and his hand was around her neck, squeezing the life out of her.

By the time he was finished raping her, she was dead. He tossed her body in the ditch alongside the road, then made his way back to his car, singing as he went.

CHAPTER 2

The Goldline passenger train sped down the tracks noisily, drowning out the sound of the music they were pumping through the speakers. The sun was just beginning to rise in the sky and some of its rays danced playfully through the windows of the train.

Scott Sharp was sleeping when the rays began to beat down on his face. His eyes fluttered open, and he looked out the window. The countryside flew by as the train made progress to its next destination. It was quiet on the train, and if the sun hadn't come, Scott may have slept right through the next stop. He was hungry and decided last night that he would eat in the town of Burdensville.

Scott had been traveling for nearly a year on his own, ever since Kelly had died. Kelly had been his wife for two years and his girlfriend since high school. She had been funny, smart, and breathtakingly beautiful, but the cancer had robbed her of those things. When she finally passed, after all they had been through, he felt more relief than grief, and the guilt of that fact made looking in the mirror unbearable. He took off, giving up their cute little bungalow, and began to go wherever the road took him. He would know when the time was right to stop and go home.

As of today, the time still wasn't right. He rubbed his eyes as he tried to force the image of his Kelly out of his mind. His stomach growled loudly, giving him something else to think about for a split second. It didn't matter though; his mind was back on Kelly in no time at all.

∞

"Scott, I went to the doctor for my yearly physical today," she had told him over supper.

He scooped some mashed potatoes on his plate. "Yeah? How did it go?"

Kelly had begun playing with her food. When she didn't respond right away, he looked up at her; she had a tear running down her face.

"Kelly, what is it?"

She cleared her throat and wiped her eyes. "He found a few lumps."

Scott absentmindedly put his fork down, his eyes not leaving her face. "What do you mean, he found a few lumps?"

Kelly sat back in her chair. "I have an appointment with the oncologist on Monday at Coos General for a biopsy."

"So, it could be nothing, right?" he asked.

Kelly had shook her head. "I don't think so."

Kelly's mother, aunt on her mother's side, and one of her sisters had all suffered from breast cancer. Her sister had just had a mastectomy done last year, but her mother and aunt were both gone, victims of the horrible cancer. Kelly knew that the chances of the lumps being 'nothing' were little to none.

"I don't want to get all worked up, though. It could still be early enough to stop," she picked up her fork and continued to play with her food. Scott could tell by the sound of her voice that she wasn't convinced.

He had stood up and walked over to her, where he knelt on the floor beside her. He stayed there, holding her while both of them cried. He knew that no matter what happened he wouldn't leave her side.

Kelly sat back finally and looked him in the eye. "Don't leave me, Scott."

"Oh, Kelly," he had replied. "I will never leave you babe. Never."

∞

The porter appeared in the car's doorway. "We will be stopping in Burdensville in approximately ten minutes, ladies and gentlemen. For those of you continuing on, you will have a ninety-minute window to eat or shop before we re-board. Thank you for riding Goldline."

As quickly as he appeared, he disappeared, and Scott looked around the car. Ladies and gentlemen? There was only he and one other man in the car. The porter must have been as tired as Scott felt. He stood and went to the tiny restroom, where he relieved himself and splashed a bit of cold water on his face. He gave his armpits a whiff and satisfied that he didn't stink to high heaven, he went back to his seat, where he grabbed his two bags from overhead and put them in the empty seat next to him. He could leave them on the car but considering that the contents were all he had in the world, he would take them with him.

The train began to slow as it neared the station. Scott had his face practically up against the glass window. The town looked pretty small to him. He was from Coos Bay, which had more than fifteen-thousand people. He guessed that Burdensville had only a small fraction of that. He hoped he could find a place to eat with half-way decent food.

He stayed seated after the train had come to a complete stop and allowed the other passenger to get off first. He then grabbed his two bags and left the train. The sun hit him hard, but it felt amazing. He put his face upward towards its rays just to soak up the wonderful energy it provided.

After a moment, he looked around. Scott was standing on a wooden platform, just like the kind one sees at train stations in movies or on television. It made him smile; quaint, he thought.

Now he gave his surroundings a closer look. The main station was a small, rectangular-shaped building that ran the length of the platform. A large navy blue sign with bright orange letters was over the double doors that led inside. It read 'Burdensville Station'. From where Scott was standing, it seemed to be the only building in town, but he knew better. It was just blocking his view.

He walked to the double doors. On the left door was a white hand-written sign which read 'No Firearms Past this Point: If you plan to shoot you'll get the boot'. He chuckled. How original.

On the right door were the hours of operation for the station, and he noticed that it was open only three days out of the week. Those days must've been the only ones when a train actually stopped.

He grasped the door and swung it open, stepping inside. There were two rows of four metal folding chairs which faced the large picture window that overlooked the platform. A soda machine and another with chips and candy bars was on the left wall, as was a change machine. The wall across from him sported several maps of the area. Next to that was a large cork bulletin board which had several missing person notifications on it; all three of the victims were women, and they had all been stamped as cancelled. This signified they had been found, and he wondered why they were still hanging. This place must be full of slackers, he thought to himself. He raised his eyebrows and began to make his way over to have a gander.

There were three of them in all, and all of the people missing were young women. He shook his head in disbelief as he scanned them. Surely, these women were missing from surrounding towns. Burdensville probably didn't even have that many women living there on a day to day basis. On further inspection, he discovered he was right; they all had been passing through. He wondered if they had been found dead or alive.

Now he turned to the right. There was another door which led out to the town itself, and along the right wall was a window with a skinny old man behind it. He was reading a worn copy of a magazine through a pair of narrow reading glasses. Scott approached the window.

"Excuse me," he began. The man looked up at him over the top of his lenses, and he didn't look too pleased that he had been interrupted. "Is there a café here where I can grab a bite?"

The old man sighed in frustration and jerked his head to the right. "Ayuh. Down the road two blocks. Dickie's Café, it's called." He went back to his magazine as if Scott had already left.

"Thanks for your time," Scott replied with a roll of his eyes, hoping the man heard the sarcasm in his voice, but if he did, he gave no hint to such. Obviously, they didn't take too kindly to outsiders here.

He walked outside and walked down three steps. There, he stopped and looked around. From where he stood, he could tell that Burdensville was only about three or four blocks wide, but it seemed to go on forever in the distance. He would guess the town had a couple thousand people living there at the most. He could see a hand-painted sign on a brick building a couple blocks away: Dickie's Café. His stomach growled as though it were angry with him for neglecting it. He looked around to see if anyone had heard the noise, but he was alone. He laughed to himself.

The train station was situated at the dead end of a road which appeared to run right down the middle of Burdensville. The road was made of hard dirt and gravel. The right side had no sidewalk; the houses on that side seemed to have yards that ran right to the road. The left side, however, did have a narrow sidewalk, and Scott could see that it ran right by Dickie's Café and continued on. He walked across the sparse train station lot and started up the sidewalk, which was crumbling in disrepair. Tufts of grass and weeds grew in the cracks and in some spots, the concrete of the sidewalk had buckled severely, making it potentially dangerous to even walk on it.

It was technically two blocks to Dickie's Café, but they couldn't really be called 'blocks'. In reality, there were two streets to cross, but each block had only two houses on it that faced the road. The houses were old and massive; a couple of them had yard decorations and old ladies kneeling in flower beds that reeked of perfection. One home had a middle-aged man using a manual push mower on his lawn, and another had a rusty old swing set in front.

As he walked, he took it all in. He noticed that his presence had sparked a bit of interest in the locals. As he would pass, they would stop what they were doing and stare in his direction. The man with the mower managed a half-assed wave, but his eyes were filled with both curiosity and distrust. Scott waved back and said under his breath, "You would think, they aren't aware I got off the train…" but he was sure they were just nosy.

In no time he found himself on the sidewalk in front of the café. It had a single glass door with an 'open' sign hanging in it. A bell dangled, next to the sign, inside the door. A large red and white striped awning hung in tatters over the door. Scott reached out and grasped the door handle and swung the door open.

The bell jingled to announce his presence, and as if on cue, everyone in the restaurant went silent as they turned their attention to him. He smiled and nodded, looking from one person to another. The place was packed; it was likely the only place these hicks had to hang out, and he felt sorry for them at the thought.

A long Formica counter with padded stools was on the opposite side of the room. A waitress stood behind it cutting a slice of pie. Another waitress with ample hips and swollen ankles stared at him as she warmed up a customer's coffee.

Scott nodded at them all again and made his way to one of the stools at the counter. He put his bags on the floor and took a seat, grabbing a single laminated card that served as the menu for the establishment. One glance told him they served the typical café fare; he would be able to fill his belly here, all right.

"Can I help you?" The waitress behind the counter was now putting the pie into a cooler. She was in her early twenties and had a very friendly face that was free of makeup. She bordered on beautiful, but her tired eyes and unembellished countenance kept her appearance pretty 'run of the mill'.

Scott smiled at her. "So, what's good here…" he looked at the plastic name tag over her left breast. "Denise?"

She didn't return his smile. "If you're hungry enough, anything is good."

He searched her face for only a second, then said, "I guess, I'll need a few more minutes."

"Suit yourself." With that she grabbed up a plate with a fresh piece of pie on it and headed to one of the tables.

Scott was pretty much a creature of habit. No matter where he ate, he typically picked the same food. If it was breakfast, he would order two eggs over medium, bacon, hash browns, and rye toast with a cold milk when it was ready. For lunch or supper, he would always have a Reuben with fries and a salad, unless the establishment didn't serve them, in which case he would have a roast beef or chicken.

Denise had returned and now she set a glass of ice water before him on the countertop. Scott returned the menu to its spot between the napkin holder and salt and pepper shakers. "I would like the Reuben, with a soda on ice."

"You get two sides." Her voice was dead and had no enthusiasm. This would be a wonderful meal.

He cleared his throat. "Do you have salad?"

Denise shifted her weight from one foot to the other, and she looked like she may just die of boredom. "Our salads are nothing but lettuce."

"How about fries?" The thought of plain lettuce with dressing threatened his appetite, and he was starving when he walked in.

"Yep," she replied. "Is that all then?"

He nodded and offered another smile. "Sure, thank you."

Denise began scribbling on her pad, then she tore the sheet out and hung it on a carousel in the window that led to the kitchen. She then grabbed a plastic pitcher of water and went to tend to her tables.

Scott's eyes scanned the room slowly. Most everyone in the place was still watching him out of the corner of their eyes, but they had all resumed whatever conversations they were having when he walked in. He reached into the inside pocket of his jacket and pulled his smartphone out.

No signal. "Seriously."

He simply shook his head and put it back. Just then the bell on the door began to jingle in earnest, and the customers went silent once more. Must be the other passenger on the train, Scott thought. He turned to see.

At the door stood a man with sandy blonde hair and glasses. He was slight in build, standing only about 5'5" or 5'6", and he probably weighed only a buck fifty soaking wet. His clothes and his face were smudged with dirt, and his eyes were glazed over.

"Whassup, Neece?" The man began to cackle, as if he had just told the funniest joke he had ever heard. "Ima sittin' where I like, you see?"

The man began to stagger across the room toward Scott, mumbling to himself along the way. He was obviously drunk, and he was still five feet away when the smell of him almost knocked Scott off his stool. He got closer to the stools and took his first real notice of the stranger seated at the counter.

He stopped in his tracks, but his body swayed back and forth as he tried to keep his balance. He smiled at Scott, his teeth stained brown with tell-tale chewing tobacco stains. He closed one eye and narrowed the other as he looked the stranger up and down.

"Hoo da hell you?"

Scott was amused, but he controlled his laughter in the name of diplomacy. "I'm just passing through on the train; just here to get a bite to eat."

The man grunted and looked away. He took a seat two stools down from Scott and held tightly onto the counter before him to keep from falling off. Scott shook his head slightly and grabbed a menu to read. The last thing he wanted was to engage in conversation with this lush.

Denise appeared behind the counter and grabbed a plate from the window. She put it in front of Scott along with an iced soda she had already poured. She then turned and grabbed a small plate with fries.

"Thank you, Denise," he said with a smile.

She gave him a cold nod and then turned to the drunk. "Ronnie, what will you be having today?"

The man named Ronnie leered at her. "A little Denise with a side of... Denise." He began to laugh uncontrollably, spit flying from his mouth as he did. He almost fell from the stool but got his composure just in time to avert disaster. Scott could smell the wave of alcohol that came off of him; it was mixed with the stink of sweat and grease.

"Look, Ronnie," Denise replied. "I just don't have time for this today, okay? You can see how busy we are."

Scott tried to keep his eyes on his own plate as the stinky man processed what Denise said to him. "I jus' don' care. All these people can kiss my ass."

She seemed to tense up immediately, her shoulders squaring off and her eyes filling with dread. "You figure out what you want, and I'll be back in a minute, okay?"

She began to walk off, but the man was having none of it.

Ronnie spun around, turning a full circle before he adjusted and turned in the direction she was walking. "You know what I'll do, you lil bitch. I can make you feel good or bad. What-cha want?"

Everyone in the place began to whisper and mutter amongst themselves as they pointed and stared. Scott had even focused his attention on the situation at hand. Denise froze where she stood, and Ronnie began trying to stand.

"I'll take away your problems, lady," Ronnie slurred. "I'll throw you down and do you right. Then I'll cut you all the way from your neck to your crotch. I'll lay you open."

The customers were getting louder now, and Scott noted that no one made an effort to intervene. They all seemed to watch just to see how the scene was going to play out. He noticed that Denise had begun to shake violently, and he felt the fury piling up inside of him.

Scott stood up and put his hand on the drunk's shoulder. "Look, man, go easy on her. Maybe you need to sleep it off."

No sooner were the words out of his mouth than Ronnie swung a roundhouse at him, his fist connecting solidly with Scott's mouth and chin. Blood filled his mouth. He roared with anger and flew at Ronnie then tackling him to the floor. He put him in a tight headlock and punched him in the head hard a couple of times.

"Denise, this annoyance is drunk," Scott shouted. "Call the police before someone gets hurt for real!"

R.W.K. Clark

CHAPTER 3

Ronnie struggled on the floor against Scott, who held him firmly in place. "Lemme go, you son-of-a!" Ronnie yelled every profanity in the book at Scott, over and over as he squirmed and fought. As the two men struggled, the customers that were closest to them, stood up from their chairs to move away. It was a good thing, because the two of them ended up turning a couple of the chairs over.

"The more you fight me the worse it's going to get, man. Just relax!" Everyone was talking loudly now, and the entire café had gone into chaos mode. "Denise, did you call the police?"

"They're on the way," the waitress replied from behind the counter. Her voice was shaky, and it made Scott look up. She looked horrified, and tears were running down her face.

As if on cue, the bell jingled in the door, and everyone went silent yet again. Scott tightened his grip on Ronnie and looked toward the door. He saw the black patent leather shoes first. He raised his eyes to see a large, stout man with a badge and gun.

"What the heck is going on here, Ronnie?" The cop sounded frustrated, as if he had dealt with this annoyance for far too long.

Ronnie went limp in Scott's arms and tried to respond to the question, but the only thing that came out of his mouth was a loud whine. He took another breath and said, "This guy's tryna beat the shit outta me!"

Now the cop, whose badge read 'Burdensville Sheriff', kept his eyes glued on the two men. "Denise! What's going on?"

Denise remained silent. Scott shifted his eyes to her, but she was looking at the ground, as though both afraid and embarrassed. What is wrong with these people?

"Sheriff, my name is Scott Sharp," he began, his voice grunting from the effort of controlling the drunken idiot he was dealing with. "I'm just on a layover from the train. This guy is drunk and he threatened to not only rape that waitress, he threatened her life as well." Ronnie began to struggle harder, spit flying from his mouth.

The sheriff didn't acknowledge Scott at all, he just got quiet. He looked the two men over and said, "Is that right, Ronnie? Is this guy speaking the truth?"

Ronnie grunted and relaxed a bit. "I ain't done nuttin'."

Scott continued. "He's putting up a heck of a fight. If you cuff him, I'll let you have him, but he's being pretty damn violent."

Ronnie twisting his arms in a wasted effort to break free of Scott's hold. They began to struggle together once again.

The sheriff remained still, choosing only to observe the two men on the floor. His arms were crossed over his chest, and he was shifting his weight from one foot to the other as he considered the situation at hand. He chewed thoughtfully on a toothpick he held in the corner of his mouth. He didn't pay Scott too much attention, though; he was too busy staring at Ronnie with a frustrated look on his face.

Finally he spoke, but he still did not make eye contact with Scott. "Let him go, son."

Ronnie immediately relaxed, as if on cue. Scott looked at the sheriff, confused. Wasn't he even gonna cuff this crazy guy? The sheriff made no motion for either the handcuffs on his belt or the gun in the holster on his hip. Well, Scott finally concluded, he knows this annoyance better than I do.

With that he released his hold on Ronnie, who jumped up faster than someone whose butt had been burned. He ran his hand through his hair with a shaky hand and started chuckling. "You dumb," he said to Scott. "You done butt your nose in the wrong bidness, ayuh!"

No sooner was Ronnie free than the sheriff took his cuffs off his belt. He looked at Scott, making eye contact with him for the first time since he got to the café. "Put your hands in the air and turn around, stranger."

At first, Scott thought the sheriff was talking to Ronnie. He looked at the erratic man, who was still laughing, now even harder. Scott smirked at him with satisfaction.

"I'm talking' to you, boy," the sheriff said with a quiet but stern voice.

Scott looked back at the cop, confusion all over his face. "Me? You're saying you want to arrest me?"

"Put your hands up and turn around now, or I'm gonna have to use force," the sheriff replied.

"What do you mean?" Scott asked incredulously. "Everyone in this place saw everything!" He began to look around at the crowd, which had gone completely quiet. Each and every one of them was staring at the floor nervously. Even Denise kept her eyes down as she fidgeted, anxiety all over her face. "Waitress? I mean, Denise?" Scott begged her with his eyes, but she wouldn't even look at him.

Defeated, Scott put his arms in the air and turned his back toward the cop as he had been asked to. "This is just so wrong! I was trying to help the lady and this guy assaulted me!"

The sheriff approached Scott and began to frisk him for contraband. "It's gonna go a lot better for you if you just don't talk, son." He put the cuffs on the man and adjusted them with the key so they wouldn't tighten on him. "I'm gonna take you downtown and book you, and as soon as the judge is back in town, he'll set a bond or he'll go ahead and sentence you, whatever His Honor sees fit to do."

Now Scott turned back to the sheriff. "But my train is supposed to leave in a half-hour!"

Now it was the cop's turn to chuckle. "That wouldn't be my problem now, would it?"

Scott's head was spinning. What just happened here? He began to look around the room once again, looking for anyone to have his back, but everyone in that place was acting like they were deaf and dumb monkeys. He finally shook his head and gave a resigned sigh. "The bags by the stool are mine. Please don't leave them here."

Ronnie began to laugh hysterically as he backed his way to the main door and reached behind him to open it. The bell gave a jingle and the guy backed out onto the step. "Yep, you done butt your nose in where it don't belong!" With that he let the door swing shut and disappeared from sight.

Scott looked back at the sheriff, who had taken his arm in a firm grip. Denise was at the stools picking up his bags, which she brought to the cop. "Here you go, Sheriff Darby," she said shyly, still not looking the lawman in the eyes. "Do you want me to carry them to your car?"

"No, Denise," he replied. "I walked over here, so I expect you can bring them down to lockup after your shift, if you kindly would."

"No problem sir," she said. She then went around to the other side of the counter and put the bags there for safekeeping. Finally, she looked at Scott, her eyes full of remorse. "Don't worry, Mister. I won't let anything happen to them."

Scott just shook his head, and with a jerk to his arm by Sheriff Darby he was led out of the café and into the sunlight.

"I reckon you'll want to be knowing how often the judge comes," the sheriff said as they started walking up the sidewalk.

Scott gave a sarcastic laugh. "Yeah, I suppose I would."

"Well," the cop replied, "He comes twice a month, once every two weeks. He was just here last Wednesday, so you'll have a week and a half to wait, son."

Scott stopped, his mouth agape. "A week and a half? Are you kidding me?"

"Now I'd be watching your mouth, boy," Sheriff Darby retorted, his eyes flashing. "You can't just go around from town to town and assault the citizens who live there. This is what happens." He gave Scott's arm another jerk and they started walking once again.

"Sheriff, that Ronnie guy assaulted me! He hit me! Don't you see the blood all over me?" Scott said with exasperation. The sheriff just kept pulling him along, and they took a right at the next corner.

About half a block away was a brick building that was about the same size as the café. A sloppy hand-painted sign hung over the door:

City Hall

Sheriff

Jail

Scott was relieved. The handcuffs were cutting into his wrists a bit. He couldn't wait to get them off. He stood next to Sheriff Darby, who had a firm hold on his upper arm as he shuffled through one of several keys on a key ring. He soon found the right one and unlocked the door, after which he shoved Scott inside first.

"You have a seat right there, son," Darby said. "I'm gonna grab some booking paperwork so we can get you signed in."

Scott did as he was told, sitting forward in the chair so his hands, which were behind his back, didn't get smashed and hurt him worse. He looked around the room, taking in his surroundings. The room reminded him a bit of the jail on "The Andy Griffith Show". Along the back wall were two cells separated by a cinder block wall. Each cell had a toilet, sink, and flat metal bed with a mattress folded in half at the foot of each. There were two desks in the room: the one before him, which had a nameplate reading 'Sheriff Robert Darby'. It was piled high with paperwork and dust. Another desk was situated directly across from the first, and Scott had to turn around a bit to see it. It was much neater than the sheriff's, with only a telephone and two stackable boxes marked 'In' and 'Out'; both were empty. There was another nameplate on this desk which was marked 'Honorable Rupert Allen. This desk had a thick coat of dust on it that hadn't been disturbed in some time. Scott groaned and rolled his eyes before hanging his head in frustration.

Sheriff Darby sat down hard in the chair at his desk, grunting as he did so. In his hand were a few sheets of paper, and he laid them on his desk before taking the first one and winding into a cast iron typewriter that had to be older than both of the men sitting there.

"So, Mr ..." The sheriff began.

"Sharp," Scott replied. "Scott Sharp"

The sheriff began pecking at the keys. "Middle initial?"

"W," Scott said.

Peck, peck, peck.

"Birthdate and social security number?" The sheriff glanced at Scott and then turned back to the typewriter, fingers poised impatiently over the keys.

Scott gave the information, and as they went through the process of filling out the paperwork, he decided that he would be as cooperative as possible, no matter how angry he was. The fact was that this was a very small town, and no one here was going to be on his side. It would be like shooting himself in the foot to be rude, sarcastic, or combative.

The third piece of paper was for his fingerprints, which he gave eagerly because the handcuffs were finally removed. He then allowed Darby to take his mug shot, after which he was given a navy blue jumpsuit, which was two sizes too big, and some bedding and a pillow. Sheriff Darby then locked him securely in the first cell.

"I suppose, you'll be wantin' a toothbrush?"

Scott looked at the cop in disbelief, but he didn't voice his thoughts.

"I'd appreciate that, sir."

Darby went into a closet and brought back a towel, a washcloth, a small bar of soap, and a toothbrush. "Don't have paste, so you're gonna hafta make due."

Scott took the items and put them on his bed; then, he turned back to Darby. "I just want to clarify, sir. I will be here for the next week and a half?"

"Yep," Darby replied as he pulled a toothpick from his chest pocket and tucked it into the corner of his mouth.

"At least. Maybe longer, though. It depends on whether or not Judge Allen has more important cases on his docket. You'll just have to cool your jets and be patient. Now, I'll bring you some supper from the café around five or five thirty. I don't take orders; what you get is what you get. You will be here alone most of the time, so you'd best get used to the silence around here."

Darby plucked his hat off the lamp on his desk and put it on. He then, grabbed the paperwork on Scott and placed it in a manila envelope, which he in turn, put on the blotter on his desk.

"Well, I'm outta here then," he said in a gruff voice. "I'll see you at dinnertime."

"Wait!" Scott went up to the bars and put his face as close to them as he could. "Don't I get a phone call, or get to talk to a lawyer?"

Darby turned around, his eyes flashing. "This here ain't like the big city, boy. We don't have the manpower to let you have all kinds of 'big city' privileges. You'll get a call when I have time, and then only one, so you'd better use it wisely." With that he walked out the door, and Scott could hear him lock it from the other side.

He plopped down on the thin plastic mattress and put his head in his hands. "What the heck am I gonna do?"

He knew he had to think of something, but he was at a loss. All he could do was wait for Sheriff Darby to return and hopefully he would get a call. He wanted to bail himself out; he had plenty of money. But he wasn't even going to see a judge for two weeks.

He stood and made his bed, then lay down. He was going to stay calm. Causing a ruckus was only going to hurt him at this point.

CHAPTER 4

Denise Jensen stacked the last of the clean drinking glasses on the shelf beneath the counter. She then gave the countertop one last wipe down before turning to Dickie, who was sitting in one of the booths tallying the day's earnings.

"If you got nothin' else for me, Dickie, I'm gonna head on home."

Dickie looked up from his paperwork and smiled at the girl. She had worked for him since her parents died when she was only sixteen. Now she was twenty-five and just as pretty as a picture. Dickie loved her like his own daughter.

"I'd like you to wait for me, if you don't mind Denise," he replied, setting his pen down on top of his notebook. He turned toward her more so he could look at her head on. "Ronnie was a bit overboard earlier, and I don't feel comfortable letting you walk yourself home."

Denise hated to look weak or dependent, but she was relieved by his offer. "That would be fine," she said as she put her jacket on. "Actually, I couldn't be more pleased."

Dickie nodded and went back to his paperwork. Denise walked up to the big window on the side of the room and looked out into the night. Ronnie had really freaked her out today. She had seen him behave badly on numerous occasions, and Sheriff Darby always seemed to catch him when he fell. He was considered, by most everyone, to be the town idiot. He was always getting drunk and threatening people, but this was the first time she had ever seen him actually get violent.

It was also the first time she had watched the sheriff arrest someone who didn't deserve it just to take the focus off Ronnie. She just couldn't understand him going that far but after saving Ronnie's hide time and again maybe he just didn't know what else to do, given the situation with the stranger and all.

"Dickie, why do you suppose Sheriff Darby arrested that man from the train?" Denise continued to look out the window, but she was also watching Dickie's reflection in the glass. His pen froze over his paper and he looked at her in silence.

She turned around to face him. "I mean, everybody here knew that the stranger had done nothing wrong," she continued. "We all saw Ronnie punch him! None of it makes any sense."

Dickie laid his pen down and sat back, crossing his arms over his chest. He cleared his throat. "You know, I've lived here in Burdensville my whole life, just like you. Darby has always had a weak spot for Ronnie, almost like he feels obligated, but the only one who knows why is Sheriff Darby himself. Maybe he feels sorry for him because he's so off. I mean, Ronnie Smith is as crazy as a jaybird, and he can't be trusted. I suppose, someone has to have his back."

Denise nodded and turned back to the window. She thought about Ronnie and the things he said to her. A chill ran up her spine as she considered the threats and harassment from earlier that day. Then, she thought about the murders.

In the last two months, Burdensville had a few unsolved murders. Each was a young woman, all of them strangers to the town. They had passed through, each one, and then their bodies had been found shortly thereafter. The latest body had been a young college graduate. She hadn't been in Burdensville at all. Her parents said she had only been traveling through for a job interview, so she would have passed through, but her body was found in a ditch on a gravel road outside of town.

Whoever had killed those girls had never been caught. Denise toyed with the idea that it was Ronnie. She never suspected him before, at least, not until now, after he caused such a ruckus. Now, she found herself wondering why she wasn't suspicious before.

But Ronnie was harmless, wasn't he? The threats he had made were all just smoke. No one in town was afraid of him; they were all simply sick of his drunken behavior.

But today, suddenly, made her wonder. She shook her head hard, as if to rid it of its thoughts, then she walked away from the window and sat in a booth to wait for Dickie. She closed her eyes and leaned her head back against the window. She could feel a headache coming on.

Suddenly, the stranger came back into her mind. He sure had no idea what he was getting himself into when he came to her defense, did he? She recalled the way Ronnie punched him and how furious the man had gotten when he realized he was bleeding. She felt terrible that the sheriff had put the poor guy in jail for basically nothing at all, and she also felt strangely obligated. After all, he had been kinda cute, to say the least.

"Are you ready, Neece?" She opened her eyes to see Dickie standing there putting his jacket on. He had always been there for her when she needed him and even he knew that what had taken place that afternoon had been wrong. Regardless, Dickie hadn't come out front from the kitchen to protect her. Nobody in Burdensville liked to cross Sheriff Darby when it came to Ronnie Smith; nobody.

She smiled at Dickie and pulled her tired body out of the booth. "Thanks for walking me home. We'll have to drop that man's bags off down at the jail, I hope you don't mind. I could've walked myself, but I have to admit that having you with me makes me feel better."

"Well, Ronnie's an unpredictable so-and-so, girl," Dickie said, shaking his head. "You know as well as I do that not-a one person in this rinky-dink town trusts him behind their back."

Denise zipped her jacket and followed Dickie out the front door, letting him shut off the lights and lock the place up. "I know, but none of us have ever seen him hurt anyone. He has never hurt anyone that I know of, anyway."

"No, but we all know he's unstable, and you know what that means." Dickie finished locking up and offered Denise his elbow. "Shall we depart, Madam?"

"Oh, thank you kind sir," she replied, offering him a curtsy. Together they began walking to their homes with only the street lights guiding them in the blackness.

Dickie talked during the entire five minute walk. He told her he was going to take her home first, then he would drop the stranger's bags off to Sheriff Darby. Then, he talked about his oldest daughter who lived and worked in Sacramento. He talked about how he hated her 'holier than thou' attitude and how she alienated him and her younger sister. He talked about how the younger sibling was such a mess, taking drugs and hitchhiking all over the United States. It worried him sick.

"Well, here we are, Neece," Dickie said, walking the girl to her front door. He stood by as she unlocked the door. "I'm not leaving until you are secured inside there, got it?"

Denise smiled at her boss and stood on her tiptoes to kiss his whiskered cheek. "Thank you, Dickie. I don't know what I'd do without you."

"Well, now. You had better figure it out. I won't be around forever, you know."

She patted his cheek after kissing him and then went inside, closing the door and locking it behind her. As soon as it was locked, she leaned against it and took a deep breath. What a relief to feel safe; she had been on the edge of her nerves ever since the incident with Ronnie and the stranger at the café.

She hung her jacket up on a hook by the door and dropped her purse on a small table next to the front door. Denise made her way down the short hallway where the bedrooms and bathroom were. She opened the door at the end of the hall and held it open just enough for the hall light to shine in. Her sister, Diane, was curled up under her blanket sleeping peacefully. Denise smiled in spite of herself; her kid sister was the light of her life. She could only hope to do right by the teenager because she had no idea what she was doing.

She went back out to the living room and kicked her shoes off before going into the kitchen for a bite to eat. She chose a piece of cold chicken and pulled it apart to make a sandwich. She was hungry and exhausted. What a day it had been! Ronnie was trouble, but he had never spoken to her in that way her whole life, and she had known him that long. She put a handful of chips on her plate with the sandwich, poured a cold glass of milk, then went out and plopped on the couch. She turned the television on, and the news greeted her loudly. She quickly turned it down a couple of notches so the noise wouldn't disturb her sister's sleep.

"The latest news about a young woman's body found outside of Burdensville has nearby communities feeling unsettled, to say the least. According to the victim's family and friends, Carly Reed was heading to an interview for a teaching position," the anchor was saying. "When she didn't arrive and no one had heard from her, she was reported missing. Her car, a 2001 Beetle, was discovered ten miles outside of Burdensville with no sign of the girl. Her body was discovered only two miles outside of the town. The state medical examiner claims that the injuries discovered on the body were consistent with those on, at least, five other rape and murder victims in the last couple of years. Miss Reed had a crushed larynx and had been violently sexually assaulted. Burdensville police are investigating that murder, as well as the others, in cooperation with local police. We will keep you posted on any updates as we get them."

Denise shut the television off and tossed the remote onto the coffee table. Her mind was going in circles. Everyone in Burdensville had been on edge because of the murders, and Sheriff Darby was none too eager to share information with the locals. It had to be someone either living in Burdensville or nearby. It made her stomach ache just thinking about it. For all she knew, it could be Dickie himself.

Denise stood up and made her way to her bedroom. She hadn't been scheduled to work tomorrow, but Donna had an important doctor's appointment in the city, so she had agreed to fill in for her. It didn't bother her; she could always use the money, but she had to admit that she was terribly behind on her yard work. She had asked Dickie numerous times if he was ever going to hire a third girl, but he always dodged the topic. He said that she and Donna were all he needed, and so far he had been right, but neither of them rarely got a legitimate day off.

She focused on eating her food, then turned off the lights and went to bed. She stopped in the hallway at Diane's room once again. The murders made her nervous. What would she do if something ever happened to Diane? The thought was petrifying. Taking care to not make noise, she turned the knob and opened the door just a crack, letting the same sliver of light shine on the figure sleeping peacefully in the bed once again. From where she stood, she could now see the figure's chest moving up and down as it breathed. She smiled, satisfied, and closed the door.

Her sister Diane was all she had left, and she wanted to do nothing but keep the girl safe and sound. She was seventeen, and she would graduate from high school this year. She planned to study nursing and had already been accepted on full scholarship to Central Medical Center School of Nursing. She was at the top of her class, and she was highly gifted and beautiful.

Denise had taken responsibility for Diane when their parents were killed. Diane had been only eight at the time, and Denise had to quit school and start working, but it had been worth it. The girl was going to go places. She was going to get out of Burdensville and be somebody; Denise was going to see to it even if it took the life out of her trying.

She went to the bathroom and brushed her teeth and washed her face, then went to her room and climbed into her bed eagerly. It felt like sheer heaven to be off her feet, and she smiled and moaned out loud, in spite of herself. She tossed and turned for a couple of minutes before she gave way to her dreams; dreams of a faceless man chasing, raping, and murdering someone that looked a lot like her.

∞

Sheriff Robert Darby locked the door of the jail securely after looking in on the prisoner. With the guy being a stranger in town, he felt he had to take special precautions, but not because the guy was a hardened criminal. Heck, he hadn't even broken any laws.

No, he just needed to make sure that the guy was more than ready to leave when the time came. In a tiny community like Burdensville, the people had their set ways, and Sheriff Darby was no exception. The last thing any of the locals needed was to have their lives disrupted by some strange guy that Ronnie had pissed off. It was just that kind of guy that could upset everything.

Darby would make sure that the trumped up charges didn't stick. He would just play dumb until Judge Allen came to hold his hearing, then he would say he had re-evaluated the evidence and decided to drop the charges. By then, this guy would be willing to leave town running, and that was what Darby wanted.

"Hey, Bobby," a voice said in the darkness, and Darby turned around to find Dickie. He was carrying the prisoner's personal effects; he had forgotten all about the bags and was relieved that Dickie had remembered to bring them by.

"Thanks, good buddy," he replied. He unlocked the jail door and placed the bags on a chair just inside. He locked up once more and turned to the café owner. "Sorry about Ronnie this afternoon," he continued. "Hope it didn't shake up people too much."

"Well, it didn't hurt business if that's what you mean," Dickie replied with a grin. "But it helps that I'm the only eatery for miles."

Darby laughed. "Ayuh, I suppose it does now."

Dickie cleared his throat. "I wondered if I could ask you a question?"

The sheriff stopped to focus his attention on the man. "You can ask me anything, so shoot."

"Why did you arrest this poor bastard, anyway?"

Darby paused for a minute. It appeared he was weighing his words carefully. Finally he said, "You know as well as I do that Ronnie ain't really got no one.

I mean, Doc Smith don't really have time for his own brother, so I feel an obligation to protect him. I mean, the guy's a damned idiot. If he can't depend on townsfolk, who can he depend on? If I arrest him and let the charges drop, he's much more likely to go quietly, you see?"

Dickie heard the words but to him it sounded like a crock of bull. Who was he to say a cross word though? Burdensville was Darby's town, and it had been for years. In general, Darby had always been a good cop, so Dickie figured he shouldn't second guess the guy's motives.

He gave the sheriff a pat on the shoulder. "You know what you're doing Darby. What the heck do I know? I just sling hash for a living."

The two men finally parted ways. Darby went to his police cruiser and forced his fat frame inside, then ran out of breath struggling to put his seat belt on. Once that was done, he was on his way. He needed to talk to Ronnie; he wanted to hear that moron's side of things even though his entire version would likely be a lousy excuse and just lies. Ronnie didn't know any other way.

He drove down the main street heading away from the train station. Ronnie lived in a breezy shack, a mile out of town on the first gravel road. As a matter of fact, the shack had once been owned by Darby's parents and when they died they left it to him. He let Ronnie live there free of rent. Lord, if he didn't look out for that retard, no one would.

He took a right on the gravel road; the shack was about a half-mile down. Darby felt an obligation to keep an eye on Ronnie, and he had his reasons. Sure, it was wrong to keep letting the guy screw up over and over and then shift the blame to the people he hurt, but Darby couldn't live with the alternative: the guilt of blowing off what he felt was a responsibility. If he didn't look out for him, no one would.

Darby pulled the cruiser into Ronnie's overgrown gravel drive and parked it behind Ronnie's beat up 1972 Grand Prix. That car used to be Darby's. He had wanted to restore it, but Ronnie didn't have transportation, and Darby gave it to him as a gift one Christmas.

He shut the cruiser off and heaved his large frame out of the car. Darby took off his hat and wiped the sweat from his forehead with his shirt sleeve. Getting in and out of the cruiser was getting harder every day. Maybe he should cut back on that pie Dickie made at the café.

"Ronnie! It's Robert! You come out here now, boy!"

He looked around and peeled his ears, but the place was dead quiet. Darby shook his head. The poor miserable pain in the neck was likely passed out cold. Well, it was time to wake him up. They needed to get a few things straight... again.

Darby put his hat back on his head and hiked his pants up before heading to the beat up old house. He hadn't been here in a few weeks, and the place looked abandoned thanks to the overgrown grass and greenery.

He knew Ronnie wasn't capable of being responsible; he would have to get out here and clean the place up for him.

The front door had been out of use for years, so Darby automatically headed for the back. He grabbed the knob and tried it; the door opened easily with a loud creek. He poked his head inside and was hit with the smell of rotten food and garbage.

"Ronnie! It's Robert! Wake your butt up, now. We need to talk!"

Suddenly, Darby could see him. He was peeking around the corner from the living room, quietly watching Darby, trying to see if he was angry. Darby smiled at him and relaxed his shoulders.

"Now, don't you be hidin'. I'm just here to talk to you, Ronnie." He opened the door all the way and stepped inside the filthy kitchen. Flies were everywhere, their buzzing terribly loud.

He removed his hat and looked around. "Jeez, Ronnie, we're gonna have to get someone out here to help you clean this place up, aren't we?"

Ronnie nodded slightly and came around the corner, his hands trembling and his eyes full of trepidation. Darby could tell the man was no longer drunk. He had a look of fear and regret that was so tangible Darby could've cut it with a knife.

"Look, Ronnie," Darby began. "I didn't come out to hassle you, but the two of us gotta have a heart to heart, understand?"

"I… I didn't mean to scare Pretty Denise, Robert. I was just havin' me some fun for a bit," he said, stuttering slightly. He did this only when he was scared.

Darby smiled at him. "I know that, Ronnie. Don't you think I know that?"

Ronnie smiled and began to nod enthusiastically.

Darby continued. "The problem wasn't Denise, Ronnie. She knows you. But now you done picked a fight with a stranger, a man that doesn't know you, and now I gotta clean up the mess."

Ronnie continued to nod, his smile fading slightly.

"You know, if you ever lose control around the wrong person, they're liable to lock you up but good," Darby continued, "And there wouldn't be nothing I could do about it."

Ronnie started to snivel, which tore at Darby's heart. "Listen, now. Just listen. It's all gonna be alright." He held out his arms to Ronnie to show him acceptance, and Ronnie all but ran into them.

"I didn't mean to make trouble, Robert," the man bawled. "I only wanted to have a little fun with the pretty girl."

Now, Darby held the man by the shoulders at arm's length. "Now, we both know that ain't altogether true, don't we?"

Ronnie's lower lip began to tremble and snot began to leak out of his nose; he shrugged in response and tried to look away, but Darby took him by the chin and made him look him in the eye.

"You threatened her, Ronnie. You threatened her with sex and physical harm, didn't you Ronnie?"

Ronnie shrugged again and began to kick at the cap from a milk jug that was on the floor.

"Now I done told you time and again that you can't be talking that way to the townsfolk, haven't I?"

Ronnie's toe connected with the cap and it went flying. This made him smile a bit, which frustrated Darby. "Haven't I, Ronnie?"

He nodded vigorously in response.

"Now I'm gonna do what I can to make this go away, but you need to keep your butt at home until the stranger leaves, do you got it?'

He nodded again.

"This weekend, I'm gonna come over and help you get this yard cleaned up," Darby continued. "Now, in the meantime, I want you to clear all this damn garbage out of this house and burn it in the barrel out back. Got it? You don't have to clean, just get the trash out and burn it; can you handle that?"

More nodding.

"Well, it better be done, because I don't want you leaving this house till this guy is gone, so you'll have plenty of time," Darby concluded.

He gave the man a pat on the back and reassured him that he wasn't in any trouble. He then reiterated that the garbage needed to go out, then he left. Ronnie's face was plastered to the front window as he watched Darby leave.

Darby gave the man a final wave and a smile as he backed out of the drive. "Poor stupid idiot, what a waste of my time," Darby said, and he put the cruiser in gear and punched the accelerator.

He couldn't get out and away from Ronnie fast enough.

CHAPTER 5

Scott Sharp was lying on his plastic mat tossing and turning. He couldn't get comfortable no matter how hard he tried; he had never slept on such a hard, lumpy surface in his life, even when he had camped. It didn't help matters that the plastic mattress he was lying on smelled like decades worth of old vomit. He had to breathe through his mouth just to keep from smelling it.

He had just started to doze a bit when he heard a key in the door. His eyes opened, and he sat up just as Sheriff Darby swung the door open and turned the main overhead lights on in the room. Scott squinted against the brightness and shaded his eyes with his hand.

"Hello, Mr. Sharp!" Darby seemed to be in a fairly good mood. "I've brought you your supper, just like I said."

Scott looked at the wall clock that was situated next to the bulletin board. Good thing he hadn't counted on the lawman being punctual. He actually had himself convinced that Darby wouldn't come back until morning.

Darby noticed him checking the time. "I know," he said. "I'm a bit later than I said I'd be, but I had some official business, and by the time I was finished, old Dickie had closed the café. I had to bother him at home to get you a meal."

He approached the bars and slid a Styrofoam box through the six inch slot at its center. He then held a paper cup with a lid through the hole for Scott to take. He stood up eagerly and took the items from Darby. His stomach started growling furiously as soon as he laid eyes on the items; after all, he hadn't eaten except for one French fry at lunch, and since early that morning, he had only what consisted of a donut and coffee.

Scott took the food and sat on the bed to dig in. "I know it isn't hot, but like I said, Dickie had to throw it together." Darby walked to his desk and sat down. He then put his feet up and stared at Scott as he observed the meal.

Inside the Styrofoam box was a bologna and cheese sandwich on dry white bread. There was also a small snack-sized bag of potato chips and a banana. The cup held lukewarm milk.

"It's fine, Sheriff," Scott replied, and he was surprised to realize that he meant it. The meal was obviously lacking but to him it looked gourmet. He tore into the sandwich without a second thought.

"So, I been thinkin' about your little uproar with Ronnie at Dickie's today," said Darby, breaking the silence. "I'm just wondering why you think it's okay to visit a place and get violent with the locals like that."

Scott looked up at the sheriff and searched his face as he chewed the bite of sandwich he had in his mouth. Was this guy serious? By his expression, Scott could see that he either didn't see anything wrong with the current arrangement, or he was a habitual liar and believed his own words.

He swallowed the bite in his mouth and said, "Sheriff, I didn't raise a hand to that Ronnie guy. In case you couldn't tell by my own appearance, I was the one who got hit."

Sheriff Darby sat up and put his feet on the floor, chuckling with amusement. "Well, it sure may have looked that way but not-a one person was willing to back up your version of events. Now, what is a cop supposed to think?"

Scott just stared at him, then focused his attention back on his food. He wasn't going to talk about this with Darby anymore. It was an obvious set up, at least in his humble opinion. He hadn't even been allowed to make a phone call.

"So, are you going to let me have my call?"

Darby stood up and put his hands in his pockets as he began to pace. He had a thoughtful look on his face and after a bit he stopped and turned to Scott. "I'll tell you what. You eat that food fast enough, and I'll let you get a call in, but make it snappy. I got things of my own to do, you know?"

With that Scott began to wolf the sandwich and chips down, demolishing it in record time. He saved his banana, but finished his milk in two gulps. "I'm done. Can I make that call now?"

Darby immediately approached the bars and started to go through the keys on his big hoop. "Now, don't be trying any damn funny business, boy, you got that?"

Scott nodded and smiled politely as he stood at the bars and waited for Darby to let him out. Soon, he was standing at the phone with the receiver to his ear; he didn't even know who to call, and hadn't thought about it much. Kelly had been his only family; he had put his own blood relatives out of his life for a variety of reasons. Since she died, and he hit the road, he hadn't really spoken to any of her people. He had been a loner.

Suddenly, he thought about Brian Weaver. He and Brian had been best friends through high school, and their relationship had gone strong until Kelly's diagnosis. It was likely very rude to call him after all this time when he was in need, but he had to let someone know what was happening. If the guy even had the same number.

He began to punch the numbers out on the dial pad. It would be long distance from here, but the sheriff didn't say anything when he started by dialing a one, so he continued. The phone began to ring in his ear immediately.

"'Hello?" Scott recognized Brian's voice right away, and he was flooded with relief.

"Brian, it's Scotty," he began.

The other end of the phone was silent, and at first Scott thought Brian may have hung up on him. He wouldn't have blamed him. He hadn't been a very good friend.

Suddenly Brian spoke, his voice surprised. "Scotty? How are you, man?"

Scott exhaled. "I've been alright, Brian. I know I haven't called, but after Kelly passed…"

"No, dude. No worries," his friend said. "So what's up?"

Scott cleared his throat and nervously shifted his weight from one foot to the other. "Brian, I have been traveling, as you probably knew. My train stopped in this town, and I got myself in something of a bind. I'm in jail."

Silence again on the other end. Finally Brian said, "What can I do to help, man? Do you need bail money or something?"

"No, no. I don't have a bond set. The town is pretty small, so I won't even see a judge for about ten days. I just wanted to let someone know where I was." Scott paused and glanced at Darby, who was busy chewing his toothpick and picking at his fingernails. "You know, just so I'm not winging it out here."

Brian must have heard something in his voice. "Are you okay, Scotty? What's going on? What did you do?"

"Well, I don't have an attorney, at least not yet," he replied, "so I really can't go into it in detail, but it's nothing drastic. I just wanted someone to know where I am, and that I am alive." He shook his head and closed his eyes: like anyone really cared if he was alive.

"So where are you then, dude?"

He opened his eyes once again to see Darby's eyes fastened on him. "A town called Burdensville."

"Where the heck is that?" Brian asked with a bewildered voice.

Darby stood then. "You're gonna have to wrap it up, son."

He replied quickly. "Look, I gotta go, my time's up. I just wanted you to know what was going on."

"Well," Brian said hesitatingly, "You call me if you need anything. Don't hesitate, Scott."

Scott smiled into the phone. "I won't. Thanks."

With that he disconnected the call and looked at Darby. "Thanks, Sheriff."

Darby motioned for him to head back into his cell, which he did. As he was locking him back up, he said to Scott, "So, it sounded like you lost your girl or something."

Scott sat on the bed and stared at his hands. "My wife," he said quietly.

Darby didn't answer right away, he just looked at him. Finally he said, "That's a tough break, son. A tough break." He stepped back from the cell, then continued. "I'll be back in the morning with some breakfast, and I'll let you get a shower then too."

Scott nodded as he struggled to keep the tears back. He was angry and frustrated at the lack of control he had in this forsaken situation. "Thanks."

Darby left then and locked the door behind him. He thought about Scott as he struggled into his cruiser. The guy had hit a rough spot, that much was obvious. He had lost his wife and took to the road to sort things out. Darby knew exactly how the guy felt. He had lost his own wife a while back, and now he found himself empathizing with his prisoner. Shame, he had to go to lengths like this when it came to Ronnie. At this point, he'd let the guy go if he could, but the paperwork had already been sent to the city courts.

Scott Sharp was just going to have to ride this one out.

∞

"I swear, Meri, if you keep messing with me while I'm driving, I won't let up when it's your turn," said Tim Bascom. "It's all fun and games, isn't it?"

Meri's laugh was like a melody, and Tim found himself smiling through his frustration. He was so glad to have met her; she was the cutest thing he had ever seen, with her strawberry blonde hair, button nose, and tiny body. It was amazing that she had agreed to travel with him to see their favorite band. They were playing in the city that weekend, and Tim intended to show her a good time.

Tim Bascom was in love.

"Aw, c'mon Timmy," Meri giggled. "Man up, will you?"

It was eleven at night, and they were traveling the last stretch to the city in the Mercury Tracer his parents had given him for his seventeenth birthday. Tim didn't want to stop anywhere else except for gas in Burdensville. They both agreed they would just drive straight through and save their money. They would have plenty of time to rest when they arrived.

"Hey, hand me a couple of those chips, will you?" he asked, holding his hand out expectantly. Meri soon put a stack of the chips in his palm and began to tinker with the radio.

"There's nothing but country music in these parts, it seems," she said, her nose wrinkled in disgust. "I can't wait to hear some real tuneage."

She flipped the radio off, and they continued to drive in silence. Meri laid her head back against the rest and closed her eyes. It would be her turn to drive soon enough. She wanted to get a little shut eye.

Suddenly the car began to slow down, and Meri opened her eyes to see what was going on. An old beater car was parked on the shoulder of the highway up ahead with its hood open. A man was standing in the middle of the road waving his arms back and forth.

"Damn," Tim said. "He's lucky I picked him up in my headlights. I could've killed the dumb bastard!"

Meri continued to watch the guy. "Maybe we should see if we can help. Maybe he needs a ride or something."

"I was thinking the same thing," Tim replied, and he continued to slow the car until they were able to pull right up alongside the man.

Tim rolled his window down. "Do you need some help, mister?"

The man nodded vigorously. His hair was thin and dirty, and his outdated glasses were smudged so badly that Tim could see the smudges in the dark.

"Ayuh," he replied. "I have a split in the end of my radiator hose. I just need to get the clamp off and trim the hose down, but I'm having' a hell of a time with the damn clamp."

"Well," Tim replied, "If you have the tools, I can see what I can do."

The guy continued to bob his head up and down. "That'd be great."

Tim put the car in reverse and pulled back behind the dinosaur the man was driving. He left his headlights on and turned to Meri. "You stay here. This shouldn't take too long, okay?" He smiled at her and leaned over to plant a quick kiss on her pouty little lips.

"You can't get rid of me that easy," she replied flirtatiously.

Tim got out of the car and approached the man, who was now standing on the passenger side of the car looking under the hood. He had a wrench in one hand and a hammer in the other. "See," he said, "If you look down here with the flashlight, you can see the split. The nut that needs to come off is right there." He motioned with the wrench, then handed it to Tim. "Flashlight's right there."

Tim took the wrench in one hand and the flashlight in the other and bent down to try and see the split. He aimed the light on the hose and turned his head back and forth. He didn't see a thing.

"I gotta tell you, mister, this hose looks fine to me," he said as he continued to look up the length of the hose.

The man cleared his throat nervously. "You don't say?"

Tim turned slightly to look at him. Suddenly, pain exploded in his head, and he collapsed over the car and slid to the ground. He struggled to see what was happening through the stars in his eyes. The guy was drawing back with the hammer like he wanted to hit him. Is that what just happened? Did that guy just hit me?

The hammer came down again and the last conscious thought he had was that Meri was screaming.

Meri sat in the car, panic stricken with her hands over her mouth as she screamed. She watched the man drop the hammer to the ground and turn toward her. Oh, crap, she thought. He is coming over here!

She fumbled with the door handle and after a bit of a struggle she got it open. She was out of the car and running back up the road in the direction they had come. Meri had been a runner in high school, but now she felt like her legs were bound in molasses. She continued to run and scream, "Help! Somebody help me!"

She could hear the man running behind her, and it seemed like he was getting closer. She took a sudden left into a field and after only a second she stumbled over a large rock. Meri hit the ground hard, and the wind was knocked out of her lungs. She rolled over and tried to catch her breath.

Suddenly the man was there, standing over her and smiling. He was shining a flashlight up into his own face, and Meri could see a strand of greasy hair falling across his forehead. She was horrified.

Now he shone the light directly into her eyes. She squinted as she gasped. "Now what did you go and do that for?" he asked. "It would have been so much easier on both of us if you had just stayed put."

He dropped to his knees beside her and watched her as she gasped. She started to whimper and cry, and the man began to mimic her sobs. "Oh, boo hoo hoo! Boo hoo!"

After a moment, he became tired of that game and the smile fled from his face so quickly it was as if he flipped a switch. He drew back his arm and brought the flashlight down hard on her face. Meri felt the bones in her nose and cheek break, and blood filled her mouth and nose. She couldn't see or breathe.

He hit her again and again, only stopping after he realized she didn't even look like a human woman anymore. No, she looked bloody and mangled. She was unrecognizable.

He placed the flashlight, which was amazingly still lit, about two feet from her lifeless body, making sure to illuminate her as much as possible. He then stood and began to unbutton his filthy jeans, letting them drop to the ground at his feet. He lay on top of her and smiled at her bloody face.

"See, pretty lady?" he asked her. "We were meant to be together."

The only sounds in the dark night were his grunts and groans as he used her to relieve himself.

CHAPTER 6

Diane Jensen sat on one of the benches in front of the Burdensville K-12 with her best friend Amy. "Did I tell you I was accepted to nursing school? I just got my letter yesterday!"

Amy shook her head. "You didn't call me or anything. I see how I rate. Anyway, congratulations! I love you, and I know you are going to be the best nurse ever."

Diane had wanted to study nursing for as long as she could remember. The thought of caring for people who needed her made her feel fulfilled and positive. She had volunteered at the retirement home on Buckley for the last two summers, and the nurses there had told her she was a natural. She didn't think she would be accepted, but when she got the letter she had been beside herself. Plus, she couldn't wait to get the heck out of Burdensville. She would never meet her future husband in this Podunk town.

Diane glanced down at her gold wristwatch. It had been her mother's, and it was her most cherished possession. "The bell is gonna ring in five minutes," she said as she stood up. "We'd better get going."

Just then a beat up old car came clunking up the street. When it got to the school, the driver slowed and ogled the two teens. "Hey, hey, you pretty girls!"

"Ugh!" Diane said as she turned her back on the man in the car. It was Smelly Ronnie Smith, the town clown. He was always gawking at her, and it not only made her uncomfortable, it made her sick. He always smelled bad, and his breath usually reeked of rotten teeth and alcohol. "Come on, Amy. That guy makes me nervous."

Diane Jensen and Amy hustled into the building, ready for their first class.

∞

"So, Denise, have you heard anything about what happened to that young man from yesterday?"

It was Madelyn Harris, one of the oldest residents of Burdensville. She sat at the counter of Dickie's with her sister Margaret; they were twins in their eighties. They lived together in the largest home in town, and they tried to soak up as much of the town gossip as they could at any given opportunity.

Both of the sisters had been in their yard, working in their garden the day before when the stranger was walking to the café. They practically heard about his confrontation with Ronnie Smith almost while it was happening. It was vital to keep up with the comings and goings. How else could you look out for your friends and neighbors?

Denise smiled at the ladies as she filled their coffee cups. They tickled her, the way they leaned toward her as if they were discussing something top secret, and the way they spoke in hushed tones while they looked back and forth to see who was paying them mind.

"I haven't, to be honest," she replied as she reached for a small container of half and half and set it down before them. "All I can tell you is that Dickie told me this morning that we'll be making his meals. He had to come back after we closed last night and whip something up for him."

Margaret shook her head, a look of disgust on her face. "I can't believe Sheriff Darby is holding him." She took a sip of her coffee and continued. "He should have taken Crazy Ronnie in. He should've taken that nut case in years ago."

"I'll never understand it," Madelyn chimed in. "So many times, so many things. Ronnie falls in crap and comes out smelling like a rose every time."

Denise smiled at the analogy. "I should've said something," she muttered. "It seems like anyone that approaches Darby about Ronnie ends up on his shit list. Now, I feel like a bad person for not doing what was right."

"Ayuh," Margaret agreed. "I think, we all feel the same way. None of us understand it at all. It makes no sense. But don't you go feeling bad, honey; you have Diane to worry about."

"Well, all I can say is that Darby had a younger brother back when he was but a tyke," Madelyn said in a low voice as she looked around the café. "The boy died, and as far as anyone in town knew, the Darbys never even had a service for him."

"Really?" asked Denise. "You know, I heard the same story in passing years ago, but I blew it off as hot air. Why would they not have a service?"

Madelyn replied, "Rumors have always said the baby and the mother died at the hands of the father, but he never did a second of time."

Margaret nodded. "Really! Sister and I have always believed that the sheriff has taken to Ronnie to make up for the loss, haven't we, sister?"

"Yes we have," Madelyn replied. The two old women lifted their coffee cups to their lips in unison.

Denise stared at them and turned over that tidbit in her mind. Lost a brother? "How come no one ever talks about that?"

Margaret put her cup on her saucer. "The Darbys made it clear they didn't want to discuss it, and so no one ever does."

"He started hanging out at the Smiths' house down on Dire Street shortly after that. They would give him nickels to run errands. Mrs. Smith had Ronnie, and he took a lot of care," Madelyn elaborated. "The town just assumed that Darby dealt with the grief over his brother by taking Ronnie under his wing."

Denise left the two women to their conversation and began to fill salt and pepper shakers, but her mind was on what she had just learned. How had she lived here her whole life and never heard about Darby having a dead brother? Regardless, the Harris twins were probably right; if Darby started helping Ronnie's mom, he likely formed an attachment to the boy in the process.

The bell on the door jingled gaily, and Denise and the twins all turned to see who was coming in. It was Sheriff Darby, looking rested and fresh. He had a broad smile on his face, making him appear more self-satisfied than happy.

"How are we doing this morning, girls?" He took a seat at one of the tables in the middle of the room. He never sat in the booths due to his stature, and the twins were at the counter, so he was settling for the next best thing.

Margaret gave him a big plastic smile, as if they hadn't just been gossiping about him. "Just wonderful, Sheriff. Just grand."

"Good, good," he replied. He turned to Denise and gave her a big smile as well. "And how are you, young'un? Have you rid yourself of yesterday's crisis?"

"Nothing a good night's sleep couldn't fix," Denise replied. "What can I get you today, Sheriff?"

He looked thoughtfully toward the ceiling. "Hmm. Let's see, shall we? I'm gonna need a couple of breakfasts to go. Make 'em fried eggs, taters, bacon, and white toast, will you. Oh, and a milk for my prisoner. I'll have a coffee to go."

Denise scribbled in her pad as fast as he spoke, then turned the order over to Dickie in the kitchen by means of the carousel. She poured a black coffee into a to-go cup and secured a lid on top, then took it to the sheriff. He smiled and nodded at her and took a drink. She sat down across the table from him.

"How is the stranger, anyway?"

Darby lowered the cup and searched her face as if trying to read it. "He's good, I expect. He'll see the judge next week, and if he behaves I'll request the charges be dropped." He took another drink of coffee. "I just want him to get the message that these smaller towns don't take kindly to strangers interfering and making trouble, you see."

Denise looked over her shoulder at the twins, who were sharing a newspaper and reading in silence. She turned back to the sheriff and leaned forward conspiratorially. "I gotta agree, Sheriff Darby. None of us here in Burdensville want trouble from outsiders."

Darby smiled big. Her words had obviously eased his mind a bit. "Ayuh," he replied. "We townsfolk have to look out for each other. We have to take care of our own."

Denise smiled back. "Yes. Yes we do."

She stood and fetched the coffee pot, then refilled the twins' cups as well as Darby's to-go cup. As she stood at his table pouring, the bell began to jingle again. She looked up to see two state troopers coming in.

"Just the person we were looking for, Sheriff Darby," said the older of the two. He came up to the table and slapped the sheriff on the back. "We're gonna have to disrupt your mornin', I'm afraid."

Darby looked a bit alarmed. "What's going on, boys?"

The younger cop spoke up. "Two bodies, just out of town on the highway. A young man and a young woman. Skulls split open, bloody messes. The girl's been raped. It's your jurisdiction. We need you to join the investigation, but I think it's gonna be headed by State."

Darby only missed a small beat. He stood with his coffee in hand. "Well, heck. Let's hit the road, I suppose."

Dickie rang his bell to signify that the sheriff's order was up. Denise looked and then turned back to the sheriff. "What about the food, Sheriff?"

"Damn, the food!" he replied. "I gotta get that prisoner fed. Listen, Denise, you mind takin' it to him? You can leave mine on my desk. I'll eat it later."

She nodded, trying hard not to show her eagerness. She couldn't believe she would get a chance to talk to the stranger. "Absolutely. I'll need the keys to the hoosegow though."

He immediately began to go through the keys on his ring, and soon he was handing her the key she needed. "Listen, if he says anything out of the ordinary or suspicious to you, I want a full report. Can I trust you to do that?"

"Sure thing, Sheriff." She took the key and slipped it into her apron pocket, then she turned her attention back to the three lawmen. "It's awful about these murders. I sure hope you catch whoever is hurting all these people."

The young trooper smiled at her, flirting a bit. "Oh, don't you worry yourself, pretty lady. It's just a matter of time."

The men tipped their hats and left right away, and Denise made a beeline for the window and started packing the food in a plastic bag. "Dickie, Sheriff Darby had to go to a murder scene outside of town. Donna should be here any minute, then I need to run this food to the guy at the jail."

Dickie looked alarmed. "Do you want me to do it?"

Denise shook her head. "Don't be silly, Dickie. Who would cook? The breakfast rush is right around the corner. It will only take me fifteen or twenty minutes."

"Well," he replied, sounding doubtful, "If you think you'll be alright, that's fine."

She packed the food up and warmed the twins' coffee. Donna, the other waitress, came in the door to start her shift right then. "Mornin' Donna."

"Mornin' Denise. Ready for the day?"

"I was born ready," she said. "Look, I have to run this food down to the jail for that prisoner. Sheriff Darby had to go investigate a couple more murders outside of town. I'll be back in a flash."

Donna's mouth dropped open and her eyes grew wide. "Two more murders? Good Lord! Wait, you have to tell me all about them!"

Denise zipped her jacket and grabbed the bags of food. "Have the twins tell you. I'm positive they heard far more than they let on." She smiled and winked at the older ladies, who returned her smile and waved her away.

"Come on over here, Donna Mae," Margaret said. "We have the poop."

Denise left the three women to rehash the drama, walking out the door quickly. As she walked to the jail, she thought about the news. Two bodies, likely murdered, right outside of town. She wasn't at all surprised; as a matter of fact, it was typical. Anyone could go to the train station and see how many people were missing that hadn't been found, and that was nothing compared to the number that had.

There was a slight chill in the morning air, and Denise enjoyed the way it felt when she breathed it in. She had a bit of pep in her step, which surprised her; she couldn't think of any reason to feel so good, but she did.

It took her all of five minutes to reach the jail. She set the bags down on the step and took the key from her apron. The lock opened easily, so she grabbed the bags and stepped into the musty room; it was fairly dark, the only light coming was from the few windows in the room.

She looked at the wall near the door and located the light switch. The light flooded the room glaringly, making the man in the cell cry out; he had been sleeping. The light woke him up.

Scott sat up on the edge of his bed and rubbed his eyes. It took him a moment to register her presence, and once he realized who was standing there, he was filled with surprise. What was she doing here? He jumped up and grabbed onto the bars, pressing his face against them.

"Good morning," he said.

Denise nodded. "Good morning." She walked over to his cell slowly. "The sheriff had business and he asked me to… to bring your meal."

"Thank you," he said. He felt like an idiot, but it was all he could think of to say.

She placed the Styrofoam containers on the judge's desk and removed her jacket. Scott watched her closely; she seemed to look everywhere but at him, and why shouldn't she? He had deterred that maniac at the café and ended up in jail over it. She was probably embarrassed and ashamed that she hadn't spoken up in his defense.

Denise picked up the containers and made her way over to Scott's cell. She continued to avoid his eyes as she put the containers on a folding chair and pulled it up next to him. "There is a pack of plastic utensils and a napkin inside the box," she said. She offered him a slight smile and backed away, looking around the room as if she had never been inside the place before.

Scott took the Styrofoam box and cup and maneuvered them between the bars carefully, then he sat down on the bed to eat. "So," he began, "How are you feeling since all that craziness at the café?"

Denise paced around, still avoiding making eye contact. "Oh, I'm fine," she replied lightly. "Ronnie Smith can be a bit strange, but everyone in Burdensville is used to his weirdness." She chuckled a little and continued walking around the room.

Scott took a bite of his fried eggs, which had begun to get cold. He didn't care; he was ravenous, and the food did taste pretty good. He chewed thoughtfully then looked back up at the pacing Denise.

"Well, being a stranger I wouldn't know that, but you sure looked a bit worried to me at the time." Now he watched her face for any response. She could make excuses all she wanted, but Denise had been frightened at the time, whether she was used to Ronnie's behavior or not.

Sure enough her eyes did flicker in his direction. "Well, Ronnie can exhibit some pretty… strange behavior," she replied. "I guess, it doesn't matter how long you've known him. When he's been drinking, one can never tell."

Scott nodded at her, even though she didn't see him. "I'm sure," he said. "The dude made me a bit uncomfortable. I just didn't understand how the sheriff saw fit to bring me to jail, especially now that you are telling me that this behavior is typical for the guy."

Denise finally turned and looked directly at Scott. "How is the food?" She was trying to change the subject. Scott thought he would let her.

"It's actually surprisingly good," he replied with a smile. "After only bologna for supper, I suppose, anything would have been fine."

Denise approached the cell and sat down in the folding chair. "Do you mind?"

Scott shook his head vigorously and smiled as he chewed. He finally swallowed and said, "No! Please, stay as long as you like." He took a drink of the milk and looked at her again. "So, what did you say Sheriff Darby had to do?"

Now she began to fidget a bit, picking at a non-existent hangnail. It was hard to discuss the local murders with someone who wasn't from Burdensville because no one had any answers. She supposed it was the least she could do, though.

"There were a couple of people found murdered just out of town, and the state patrol needed his assistance because it's technically his jurisdiction," she replied simply. She began to look around the room once again, and Scott didn't miss the fact. She had instantly gotten nervous.

He put his plastic fork down and wiped his mouth with his napkin. "That has to be quite an ordeal for a town this size; wow."

Denise took a deep breath and closed her eyes. She didn't want to lie to this guy; after all he had taken all this trouble on her account. The least she could do was just be honest.

She looked directly at him. "It would be, I mean, it is, but it isn't the first time. These aren't the first murders in or around Burdensville."

Scott felt his eyebrows raise. "Not the first? I mean, I don't mean to sound shocked, but typically it is much bigger cities that deal with such issues. Wouldn't you agree? You seem to not be rattled at all."

Denise laughed, surprising Scott even more. "Not rattled? I guess that's appropriate." She turned her attention back to her hangnail. "The fact of the matter is there have been more murders than you could shake a stick at, and Sheriff Darby doesn't seem to have any leads at all, at least none that he wants to tell the public about."

She stood up now and retrieved her jacket from the judge's desk. She stopped with her back to Scott and seemed to be thinking. Finally she turned around. "Look," she began. "I'm sorry about the crap that happened at Dickie's."

Scott stood up and walked to the cell door. He shook his head. "No, no," he said. "It is what it is, and from the way it sounds, you definitely have your reasons."

Denise smiled half-heartedly. "I guess, but that doesn't make it okay."

He shrugged and smiled back. "No worries, Denise."

She walked to the door, pulling the keys out of her apron as she did. She opened it and stepped out, then stopped, holding the door open. "Maybe we'll see you again before you head out of town."

"I'd like that," Scott replied.

Denise smiled once again. "Me too. I'll leave the lights on for you, okay?" With that she shut and locked the door behind her.

Scott stood at the bars of his cell for several moments, contemplating Denise and the things she had said. She certainly was a pretty one. The thought made him smile, and he even blushed a bit in spite of himself. Then he thought about the murders and the fact that Denise told him they weren't the first. This made him knit his brow a bit. That information seemed to verify what he had been thinking since he got here: something was very strange about Burdensville.

∞

Diane finished her calculus assignment and closed her book with a bang. She was glad to be finished with homework. A quick glance at the clock told her that her sister would be off work soon. The day had passed quickly, and she was tired, but she had her mind set on a hot shower and a snack before she turned in.

She began to gather her things together for the shower, and as she did, her mind went to Ronnie Smith and his catcalling that morning. Rumors about that guy had been making the rounds her entire life, and Denise always warned her to steer clear of him. That proved easier said than done, though. In a town this size, you were going to run into nearly everyone on a daily basis.

She had to admit he made her more than nervous; he actually put a literal taste in her mouth that she couldn't describe. Something inside of her was downright terrified of him. He had never done anything to deserve her judgement, but like Denise said, it was important to follow your gut in all situations. Well, when it came to Ronnie Smith her gut told her to steer completely clear.

Fifteen minutes later Diane was sitting on the edge of her bed eating a couple of chips with a glass of cold milk. When she was finished, she climbed into her bed and turned out the light. She was asleep in minutes, and Ronnie Smith was the furthest thing from her mind.

CHAPTER 7

Ronnie sat in the dust and dirt on the floor, his knees drawn up and his head against the wall. Next to him, on the floor, was a flashlight. He rolled it back and forth with his hand and watched the stream of light bounce around across the room. The light made him feel grounded and safe, especially when there was nothing but darkness, both inside of him and all around him.

His mind went to the girl in the field. He knew that she and her boyfriend had probably been found by now. When he had finished with her, he had come straight home and locked himself inside with all the lights off. A few weeks ago, he had covered all the windows with dirty towels and blankets, which added to the darkness. Funny, but the darkness, for all of its emptiness, made him feel better; it made him feel safer.

Things had gotten a little bit out of control lately; even he knew that. If they ever found out what he was doing, he knew, they wouldn't let him be free any more, but the true magnitude of that fact was unable to truly sink into his brain. He was concerned only about relieving the pressure when it came; he had no more and no less motivation than that.

The recent ones were nothing, only the tip of the iceberg. In reality, he had been doing this for a very long time. In the beginning, he would head toward the city, staying on rural roads. It was easy to get their attention. All he had to do was pretend to break down, and someone would always stop. If it was a man by himself, he would just tell him that he had help coming, but if it was a girl...

After a while, it got hard for him to go so far. He began to suffer bouts of panic with each mile he put between himself and Burdensville, and he knew what would happen if he were ever caught, so he began to hunt victims closer to home. Now he was worried that it hadn't been such a great idea. He didn't know if the boy and his girlfriend had been found yet, but they would be, that he knew for sure. The last five were just too damn close to home.

He began to cry. He was afraid of what they would do to him if they ever caught him, but he knew he wouldn't be able to stop. He had tried a couple of times, but he could never get control of the situation. It was especially bad after he drank. That was when the words in his head became loud, and the only thing that shut them up was killing. He had no choice. He felt no guilt, though. A person had to do what he had to do in this life, that much he knew for sure, and this had to be done.

His mother came to mind. When he was twelve, she had turned on him terribly. Sure, he had been naughty, and that was what caused it, but after his little brother, the doctor came along she started to treat him differently anyway. She just stopped loving him, and he hated her for it in return. When he killed the girls, he would pretend they were his mother, and that they wanted him to give them his love. Once he drained the life out of them, he could feel their love back, and it was satisfying, but only for a while.

It was as if his own mind would eat him alive. He had to relieve the nagging pain in his groin, the one that would make him pace in the filth until he did something or found someone to make it stop. Until he did that it would torture him. It would pull at him and nag at him until he got rid of it. When he was a boy, he would take pets from the townsfolk. He would do to the pets what he did to the girls now, and back then it would take care of the pain, but it didn't last, and eventually he got caught. Sheriff Darby, his good friend, had taken care of things, but he had to stop with the pets. It didn't matter to him at that point. He had evolved and he didn't even know it.

He would leave and find what he needed: sexual release. But that was never enough either. He always had to see it or feel it, the life force when it left their bodies; the look in their eyes when their life slipped away for good. Until he experienced those things, he could not stop.

He would appease the nagging pressure and feel utter relief, but it always came back, no matter how often he did things to make it stop. His mind would always begin begging for it once again, and he had no way to control it. He simply acted in the only way he knew how: according to the relief.

Now he picked up the flashlight and held it under his chin so it shone on the entirety of his face. He made a few snorting noises, which caused him to laugh. Suddenly, he realized he was laughing and his smile turned into a sudden frown. He dropped the flashlight back on the floor, and it hit the discolored tile with a metallic thud. He fished around in his front right hip pocket and brought out a small penknife. He straightened his legs and laid the flashlight on top of them so the stream of light was facing him. Opening the penknife and holding it in his left hand, he began slowly carving into the soft skin on the underside of his forearm.

The sudden pain made him gasp a bit for breath, but just like always it faded all too soon. The man shook his head in frustration as a small trickle of blood ran down his wrist. Not good enough.

Now he held the penknife straight up and down and placed the point of the blade against his skin. He began to hum as he turned it in a circle, as though he were screwing or unscrewing a screw with it. It bore into his flesh almost immediately, his blood even spurting slightly as he broke the skin and bore deeper. The sight brought him intense satisfaction.

He continued to bore into his arm with the knife, humming as he did, his teeth biting into his lower lip as he endured the exquisite pain he was feeling. Nothing he ever did made him feel so much relief. Not the murders, not the forced sex, nothing.

Soon he hit the point of release. His mouth opened and he let out a long sigh as the pain tingled, searing into his flesh. A broad smile crossed his face as a single tear ran down his cheek. His hum suddenly broke into a low song.

∞

Denise Jensen gently placed the plate of liver and onions before her customer. "Here you go, Mr. Marshall: liver and onions, green beans, and fried potatoes. Can I get you anything to go with this?"

Mr. Marshall looked his plate over, a smile of anticipation on his lips. "No, dear, I think this is just about perfect. I will take a warm up on my coffee though, ayuh."

"Sure thing," she replied as she patted his shoulder. She started up to the counter just as the phone rang. Donna answered it, so Denise grabbed the carafe of coffee off the warmer and turned around to head back to Mr. Marshall.

"Dickie's, this is Donna, how can I help you?" Donna's pleasant sing-song voice made Denise smile as she poured Mr. Marshall's coffee into his cup.

Now Donna was speaking again. "Sure thing, Sheriff Darby; she's right here. Just a moment, okay?"

Denise turned around to see Donna covering the receiver with the palm of her hand. "Denise, it's Darby. He wants to speak to you." She raised her eyebrows with curiosity, but Denise ignored the look. She put the carafe back on the warmer and took the receiver from Donna's hand.

"This is Denise, Sheriff. How can I help you?" She had plastered a smile on her face in hopes that it would make her sound pleasant, but the truth was that her stomach had sunk as soon as she heard that Darby wanted her. What could he possibly want now?

Darby cleared his throat. "Hey, Denise. How did things go with that prisoner this morning?"

"Oh!" she breathed a sigh of relief. Of course, he would want to know if things went smoothly. "Everything was fine, just fine. As a matter of fact, he was very polite. Sheriff, I really don't think…"

He cut her off. "Good, good. I was calling because it looks like I'm gonna be out here at my crime scene for quite a while. Would you be willing to take lunch to Mr. Sharp for me? Have Dickie put it on my official tab, and I'll reimburse you later on. I might need you for supper as well, if you're free."

Denise felt her heart go pitter-patter at the thought of getting to talk to Scott Sharp again. He was really good-looking, not to mention friendly, and she hadn't spent time talking to a man in years. She shook the thoughts out of her head. "Sure, Sheriff Darby. No problem. I'll take care of it for you."

"Thank you, Denise," he replied. "Like I said, I'll probably need you tonight too. I sure appreciate it, and I won't make a habit of it."

"Sheriff," Denise said, "I think you should worry about catching whoever is doing all these murders. Taking your prisoner a bite or two to eat is a small price to pay for your service, wouldn't you agree."

Sheriff Darby laughed, but to Denise it sounded a bit nervous in nature. "Sure, Denise. Sure, and thanks again." He disconnected the call without another word.

Denise looked down at the receiver in her hand and shook her head. He sure was a weird one, Sheriff Darby, but then again he always had been. Probably just under a lot of pressure over the murders.

She hung up the phone and turned to the window leading to Dickie and the kitchen. "Hey, Dickie," she said. "That was Darby. He wants me to take lunch and supper to the inmate at the jail. He said put it on the official tab, okay?"

"Sure thing," Dickie replied. "Fill out an order and send it back and I'll put a rush on it."

She fished her pad out of her apron. She didn't even need to think about it. She would order him a Reuben, and fries, just like he had ordered before he went to jail. She would also take him an iced tea with a couple of packets of sugar. Maybe it would be a pleasant surprise for him to actually get what he had ordered.

She put the order on Dickie's carousel and then asked Donna to cover her tables before checking on them one last time. By the time she was done, the order was in Styrofoam in the window, ready to go. She bagged it up and headed out, a smile on her face. She was surprised at how much she was looking forward to seeing Scott Sharp once again.

∞

Diane sat in second period Spanish, her book open in front of her, but she wasn't paying attention to it. She was tired, and being tired made it hard to concentrate. She had dreamed of her mother last night, and it had made her sleep worthless.

She dreamed of her parents often, but most of the time it was bittersweet. In her good dreams, they were all a family again, Mom, Dad, Denise, and her. They would be at the lake. She would wake from these dreams with tears on her cheeks and an ache in her heart. How she missed them both, but particularly she missed her mother.

The dream last night had been different though. In the dream, her mother had her locked in a big wooden box. Her mother would bring her food and water, and while Diane ate it, her mother was giving her a stern lecture.

"You must stay away from the animal," she had said to Diane, over and over again. "The animal will be the death of you, and I can't protect you." Diane had asked her mother what she was talking about, but her mother only began to hum a light, airy tune. It had been infuriating. Then her mother told her she would see her soon, and she walked away from Diane, leaving her in the box. Diane had cried and screamed after her mother, but the woman disappeared.

She had woken up covered in sweat. She had been crying in her sleep, and her hands were shaking violently. She got a cool washcloth and a glass of water, and soon she was calm, but she had been afraid to go back to sleep. Something about the dream gave her terror and dread, and she just couldn't deal with it.

Now she sat in Spanish and the dream was still terribly fresh in her mind. She raised her hand and Mr. Mendes responded to her.

"Yes, Miss Jensen?"

"May I be excused to go to the restroom?"

The teacher smiled and nodded, then turned his attention back to the papers on his desk. Diane left the room and made her way to the girls' room. She was going to throw up, and she didn't want to do it in the hall.

The girl actually ran the last bit to the bathroom, and she barely made it to the toilet before she vomited up her breakfast. She stayed on the floor until the nausea left her, then she flushed and went to one of the sinks. She filled her mouth with water and swished it around to get the taste of the puke out of her mouth.

Finally she looked in the mirror. Her eyes were red and her face puffy. Had she been crying again? She didn't know, but she looked terrible.

It was time to go back to class. She had only about fifteen minutes left to finish her in-class assignment. Good thing she was a straight-A student. She made her way back to class, sat at her desk, and forced herself to focus.

∞

Sheriff Robert Darby closed his flip phone and looked down at it for a long moment. He didn't feel like having Denise take the food was going to cause any problems. She knew (heck, the whole town knew) that Ronnie Smith had problems. But the fact was, and as far as they needed to be concerned, he was lifelong townsfolk, and in towns like Burdensville, well, people took care of each other.

But even though he firmly believed in Denise, and the rest of the townsfolk, for that matter, he knew that his concern was going to nag at the back of his brain like so many termites in wood until he would be able to make sure. Making sure would involve talking to someone he could trust, and with the people surrounding him right now he just wasn't free to make the right phone call. He would have to just be patient and wait.

A huge mess had been made out here on the highway. Darby slid his cell into its case on his belt, then plucked a toothpick out of his hatband. He planted it firmly in the corner of his mouth and strode back to the group of cops and investigators milling around the crime scene tape around the Mercury Tracer on the side of the highway.

Darby knew they would be out here awhile. He was basically hanging out and answering questions at this point. The state police had gotten involved in this one right away, so he was acting as a provider of information. There had been far too many recent murders in and around Burdensville in too short a period of time.

Heck. He knew things were getting very tight indeed, and he wasn't sure he even knew what his next step should be. All he wanted was for the folks of Burdensville to be safe, and that meant everybody. But now the state police and their investigators were dropping hints that Darby hadn't been doing his job. They were throwing questions at him about why he didn't feel the need to ask for help with such serious investigations. They were making subtle accusations that people wouldn't keep dying if he had. They were using words like 'negligence' and 'faulty', and it made Darby very, very nervous.

It really didn't matter in the grand scheme of things. To Darby some people were, indeed, more important than others. He had made promises and he intended to live up to them, but right now, as he stared down at the smashed skull of the young man on the road, he began to wonder if he hadn't taken his sense of obligation too damn far.

He approached the other officers with a grim smile on his face. It would be important to walk this tightrope slowly and attentively. He simply had no other choice.

But he was at the point of throwing up his hands; he'd done just about all he could do without losing complete control of the situation. He knew he couldn't just give up, though. There was far too much at risk, and what could be lost was very costly indeed, at least it was to him.

CHAPTER 8

Scott was lying on the bunk in his cell staring at the ceiling. It was so damn hot in there! He knew the weather outside wasn't the cause; the room and the cells were just stuffy, and as a result he thought he may suffocate. He had even thought about shedding the jail clothes and sporting his underwear to cool off a bit, but then he remembered that the sheriff would be bringing his lunch soon, and he chose to sweat it out.

His mind went to the waitress: Denise. What a beautiful name for a gorgeous girl! Funny, he had heard that name a thousand times in his life but it had never had quite the ring to it that it seemed to have now. He smiled as he thought about the surprise he felt upon seeing her come through the door that morning. She had sure been a welcome sight, especially when Sheriff Darby seemed to be nothing but a lying, scheming excuse of a cop.

He wished he hadn't found this trouble. He wished he had simply been able to have his lunch and talk to his waitress for a while like any normal civilian. Someone like Denise could actually get his mind off Kelly and the fact that she was gone from his life forever. The thought of his deceased wife made his stomach flip, and he had to sit up on the edge of his cot to shake it off.

Gone were thoughts of Denise the waitress; now visions of Kelly laughing were clouding his mind.

She had gone through surgery and chemotherapy, but the prognosis remained as grim as ever. Finally the day came that he and his wife had to face the facts: Kelly was going to die.

Scott made sure she was comfortable at home, and he employed a well-reputed hospice to come in and care for her so he could continue working. Each day, when he returned home, his wife would be more sickly than when he left, and with guilt he found himself wishing she would pass so she wouldn't have to live like this.

He remembered one of their last conversations. It had been a good day for Kelly; she had gotten out of bed and the hospice worker had pushed her outside in the wheelchair so she could get some air. Scott had joined her there. At first, they simply sat in silence, and he held her hand. Finally, she had turned to him, and in a weak voice she said, "Scott, you have to let me go."

He had looked at her, confused. "What do you mean?"

"I feel like I can't go. I feel like if I do, you will fall apart. You're keeping me here, Scott."

She had been toughing it out for him.

They had cried together hard that day, but Scott still hadn't come to grips with her request. About five days later, while he was at work, it occurred to him: she wanted to know he would be okay, that he would keep on keeping on. So far, he had acted like he would die when she died.

Scott went home that night, and as he and Kelly did her nightly routine to get her ready for bed, he said to her, "Kelly, I'm going to be okay. I'm going to go on. I don't know how, but I promise I will."

She had hugged him and kissed him. Then she thanked him.

When Scott Sharp woke the next morning, his Kelly was gone. Regardless of what he said, life would never be the same.

Now he squeezed his eyes shut in an effort to stop the tears, but they oozed out anyway. Here he was, in a hick town jail cell, and his situation was the last thing on his mind. All he could think about was his dead wife. She wouldn't want him to live this way. She would want him to move on and find his happiness. How could he, though? He wished he had died instead of her.

Scott heard keys in the door, and he stood up right away and quickly wiped the tears from his eyes. The clock read twelve-fifteen, so it was more than likely his lunch arriving. He wondered briefly about the person or people that had been killed, the ones the sheriff had been investigating that morning. Maybe he had already had a break in the case. Scott hoped so; no town needed the stress of having a murderer on the loose, especially a town the size of Burdensville.

The door swung open and Scott's smile grew; it was Denise bearing Styrofoam boxes. She closed the door behind her and turned to him, and as soon as she saw his grin, she returned it, adding a cute little blush to it as well. Was it just him or did she look happy to see him?

"Hi," she began shyly. "Sheriff Darby is still at his crime scene, so he called me at work and asked me to bring the food."

Scott's fingers curled around the bars of the cell, but his eyes were fastened on the woman before him. "I have no complaints," he replied. He didn't even notice that suddenly all thoughts of Kelly were gone.

She approached him with the boxes and cup, this time passing the judge's desk without stopping to put a jacket down. Scott realized, she wasn't wearing one; the day must have warmed up quite a bit. "Are the temperatures outside better than this morning?" he asked; then, he cringed. Do you really want to talk about the weather? He did a mental head slap.

"Oh, yeah," Denise said with a nod. "The mornings always seem to have a chill around these parts. Where are you from?"

"Coos Bay," he replied lightly. "We see a lot of rain and little snow, and we don't get too hot there."

"You're on the ocean, too," Denise replied. "We have to drive if we want to see it, but I never have."

Scott raised his eyebrows. "You have never seen the ocean?"

She shook her head, embarrassed. "Only in picture books." Scott made a mental note of that. He didn't know it was possible to live one's life without seeing the ocean.

Denise's smile grew, and she crinkled her nose just a bit. Scott thought she had the cutest little nose, and he found himself wishing he could plant a little kiss right on the tip of it. She was adorable.

She slid his food containers through the opening in the cell door, and Scott took them all too willingly. "What did the Good Sheriff order for me today? Bread? Water?"

The waitress gave a loud laugh and found herself wishing she had brought a 'dummy' box filled with those things as a joke. She sat down right away in the folding chair and crossed her arms over her chest. "He actually let me decide. I thought today's special would appeal to you: liver and onions." That was her best effort for teasing with him.

Scott looked up at her, struggling to hide his disappointment. He hated liver, and he always had. He knew that didn't matter at this point; he would force himself to eat it if it meant getting on Denise's good side. Ugh.

He looked away quickly to hide his disappointment and turned his attention to the boxes. She had caught the look he gave her, even though he tried to erase it from his face right away. It entertained her, and she had to struggle to keep from laughing out loud at him. Telling him she had brought him liver and onions had only been a way for her to loosen things up between them. It tickled her that she had pulled the wool over his eyes.

He sat down and flipped the top of the box back: a Reuben sandwich and fries. Now he looked back at Denise and grinned broadly. "Nice," he said. "I'm impressed. You got me."

"Well, I figured you didn't get to enjoy your order before; the least I could do was bring you what you had wanted."

Scott picked up the sandwich and took a wolf-sized bite; it was delicious! He chewed with his eyes closed so he could savor the taste. Denise's eyes scanned his face; even in jail, with mussed up hair and jail clothes on, he was quite the looker. She felt the blood rush to her cheeks, and she had to turn away.

When Scott opened his eyes, even they were smiling at her. "Thank you," he said sincerely. "I think, if the sheriff had got the food, it would have been liver for sure. After all, you said it's the special of the day."

"No problem, Scott."

The two were silent while Scott enjoyed a few more bites of his sandwich and then tore into his fries. Finally, he set the food down on the bed and looked up at Denise. "What is it with this Ronnie guy, Denise?"

She had expected him to ask her some kind of questions regarding the situation at the café that had brought him to jail. She had even considered it on the short walk over, wondering what she would say if he did. She had decided she would simply tell him the truth; nothing more and nothing less.

"Ronnie is like, well, the town idiot, so to speak," Denise replied. "I think that everyone here sort of feels like he is their responsibility, especially Darby."

Scott gave a short nod as he considered her response. "Seemed like he might be the town drunk as well."

"Well," she said, "he does have a problem with the drink, and it adds to the problems he already has. He's really harmless, though. At least, I'd like to think so. He's never hurt me or mine."

Scott's heart sunk a bit at her statement. "Are you married?"

"Oh, gosh no!" she replied. "Can you imagine the type of man I would have to marry living all my life in Burdensville?"

Now Scott searched her face, noticing that her eyes were avoiding his when she answered. "You didn't seem to think he was harmless the other day." He changed the subject back to Ronnie Smith.

Now, Denise shifted nervously on the folding chair and began to pick at the hem of her work apron. "Well, that was only because he had been drinking. You never know what's going to happen if someone is soused, you know what I mean?"

"Yeah, I guess." He took another bite of his sandwich and turned her words over in his mind. "Does he hassle a lot of the residents here?"

Denise shrugged and looked a bit thoughtful. "I wouldn't say 'hassle'; he just doesn't have social skills.

He's a lot like a kid. Sheriff Darby looks out for him, you know, takes him under his wing."

"That explains me being here," he replied.

She nodded back at him. "That's why none of us said anything; we knew it was pointless. He is just trying to keep Ronnie safe."

Scott felt the first bit of relief since coming to this forsaken town. If what Denise was saying was true, there was a good chance he would be getting out as soon as he saw the judge. The sheriff wouldn't want to prolong things. He would want Scott to leave town as soon as possible, and there was no better way to ensure this than to pop his butt in jail for a few days. He'd be more than ready to split when the time came.

He finished his sandwich, then polished off his fries. Finally, he tipped back his ice tea, without adding sugar, and gulped it all down. It was delicious.

"Thanks again, Denise," he said. "I can't tell you how much this really hit the spot."

She stood and approached the opening in the cell door to fetch his garbage. "I was hoping it would. Here, let me get rid of that for you, okay?"

He packed his cup and plastic utensils into the larger box and slid them through to her. Their hands brushed, and both of them hesitated, as if making it last as long as they could. Finally, Denise turned away in an effort to conceal the pink color that was rushing to her cheeks.

"So, do you have to get back to work right away?" Scott was gripping the bars again, looking at the waitress hopefully.

She disposed of the waste and headed back to the chair. "I can stay a few more minutes if you like. I'm sure this place is much worse if you're all alone."

Scott sat on his cot and looked at her thoughtfully. "So, you have lived here your entire life, huh? Do you have kids? I mean, you said 'you and yours' earlier, so I was just curious."

Denise nodded. "Yep. Probably for the rest of it as well, and no, I have no kids, but I have raised my kid sister."

"What, don't you want to break free? See the big world? You could take her with you!"

Now, she shook her head and looked down at her hands. She had started picking at her apron again. "Nah. My parents were killed in a car accident when I was sixteen. I've been raising my younger sister ever since, and making sure she's safe is my top priority. Traveling the world wouldn't allow me to do that." Now she looked up at Scott, her face glowing with pride. "She will be leaving next year to study nursing. I couldn't be more proud. She'll be the one to put Burdensville behind her, and I wouldn't have it any other way."

The emotion this woman felt toward her younger sibling was almost tangible to Scott. Her entire face lit up when she spoke of the girl, and he could tell that she wanted to keep talking about her. It was his pleasure to keep the conversation going. "What is her name?"

"Diane," she said, looking up at him with sparkling eyes. "I tell you, she is as smart as a whip! She will be studying at the Central Medical Center." Now she looked around the sheriff's office with disdain. She almost looked disgusted to the point of sickness. "I can't wait for her to leave this crap hole behind."

Scott raised his eyebrows, but said nothing. The hate in her voice was obvious: Denise had true contempt for Burdensville. "But if it's good enough for you here, isn't it good enough for Diane?"

She looked him in the eyes and shook her head vigorously. "I'm here for the duration, and I have accepted that. I will not accept it for her. I won't have her carrying plates to locals for Dickie, and if she stays that's what will happen." Denise cleared her throat and glanced around. "Don't get me wrong. I love Dickie, he is like a father to me. I just want more for Diane."

He could tell by her tone that she was finished talking about her sister for the time being. She even stood and looked as if she was ready to leave. "Hey," he said, trying to keep her company for as long as he possibly could, "what's up with the murders? Any word?"

He had her attention once again. She sat back down in the chair, this time on the edge of it, and she leaned forward, almost conspiratorially, even looking over her shoulder at the empty room behind her. "When Sheriff Darby called to ask me to bring your meals, he said he would be a while. He even asked me to bring your supper. That reminds me," she said as she fished her pad and a pen out of her apron, "Did you have any special requests for your evening meal, master?"

Scott threw his head back and gave a hearty laugh. He couldn't remember the last time he laughed so hard, and it felt wonderful. He looked at her through twinkling eyes and winked. "What's on the menu?"

Denise had been working at Dickie's for so long that the entirety of the menu rolled easily off her tongue, impressing Scott even more. Not only was this girl beautiful, she was smart and quick-witted as well. His heart ached at the way they had been forced to meet, but he had never been one to throw in the towel easily.

He wanted to make things easy on her, so as she rattled off the food that was available he made a fast decision and held up his hand to stop her from continuing. "How about I just go with the chicken fried steak and mashed potatoes?"

She grinned. "That's my personal favorite. Was the iced tea okay, or do you want something else?"

"The iced tea was perfect."

She tucked her pad back into her apron without writing anything on it. "Will you remember that?" he asked incredulously.

"You have no idea," she said, giving him a wink of her own. She already planned on surprising him with a slice of cheesecake.

After a moment of flirting with their eyes and smiles, Denise stood up. "I really should be going now," she said. "You're pretty good company, Scott Sharp."

"So are you, Denise… Denise…?"

"Jensen," she finished for him. "I'll be off when I come back. Do you play cribbage?"

His heart skipped a beat. "I absolutely do."

"Well," she continued, another blush filling her soft white cheeks. "Then you should resign yourself to losing a game or two this evening."

He rolled with laughter yet again, and by the time he got control of himself, she had the door open and was standing in the gap, waiting patiently. "Listen," she began, "if I don't bring you your supper, it means that Darby obviously finished up his business for the day." She looked at the ground and pushed an imaginary bit of debris with her toe. "I just wanted you to know I have really enjoyed your company."

With that she shut the door, locking it securely from the other side.

Scott plopped down on his cot and put his hands behind his head. He found himself thinking about the dreamy small-town waitress and her cute little nose. He found himself smiling at her jokes and teasing.

He hoped that Sheriff Darby would not be back before the evening meal.

CHAPTER 9

Dickie's Café was in the middle of a great big rush, and Dickie himself felt as if he was operating on total autopilot. In fact, he was, and he enjoyed the feeling immensely. It enabled him to shut out all the problems and cares of everyday life and go full steam ahead, and Dickie had plenty of problems and cares.

First, his wife was suffering terribly with chronic obstructive pulmonary disease. He had nagged her and nagged her for years to give up those damn cigarettes for good, but she had kept going, full steam ahead. For the last ten years or so, even after she started struggling to really get a good breath of air, he was sure she had continued just to spite him. But none of that mattered now. The COPD was a done deal, and now he had to work his butt off to deal with the repercussions. He loved her though, like a madman, and work his butt off he would, if it meant keeping her with him on this forsaken mudball a while longer.

Next, the bank was hassling him about late payments on his second mortgage, which he had taken out to help with Doris' medical bills. Oh, he was still paying something every single month, just like clockwork, but it was never the balance of the current payment due, or even a bit towards their past due. It just kept piling up and piling up.

In fact, the only thing in Dickie's life that was operating above the water was the café, and he wasn't about to start slacking in that department. The café was everything to him. The so-and-so at the bank knew that Doris wasn't going to be around much longer, yet they harassed him incessantly. The café was the only thing that kept him from going into complete and utter foreclosure, not to mention that working seven days a week was the only thing that kept him sane.

Today, the place was packed, more than usual. The press had barnstormed Burdensville once again with their questions and curiosities. He hated them butting their turned up noses into town business, but he supposed that was only natural. Not every tiny town on the map had a full-blown serial killer running around. But Dickie wasn't going to complain about the press, either. Their money was just as green as the next guy's.

He flipped a burger onto a toasted bun and grabbed a basketful of French fries from the deep fryer and dumped them on the plate. He put the plate in the window for Donna to pick up, along with the other three that waited there for her. As he did, he glanced out the small window: chaos, complete chaos. Dickie smiled.

Denise appeared and hung three more orders on the carousel. "Dickie, two of these are for customers that are here, but the third is for Darby's prisoner. Whenever you want to get that one done is fine with me."

A look of frustration came over his face as he grabbed the three tickets. "Denise, we're damn slammed in here, darlin'! That guy's gonna have to wait 'til folks start to clear out. I'll put the order right here," he said as he used a magnet to tack it onto the outside of a metal canister on the shelf before him. "I won't miss it. You know me." With that he turned his attention to the other two tickets and went back to work.

Denise grabbed a carafe of coffee and set about warming up cups around the place. When it got this busy she and Donna took tables individually, but they carried the entire weight of the rush together. Then, at the end of the night, they would sit down and split the tips accordingly. These were their best nights, but they tended to wear the girls out like no other. Donna was a good ten years older than Denise, but by the end of the night, Denise would feel like she was forty. She could only imagine what Donna felt like by the time she made it home.

The bell at the door jingled and three more people came into the busy restaurant. They looked like tourists, which Burdensville also got when murders happened. It was funny how seemingly normal people couldn't wait to get pictures of crime scenes, and try to steal shots of dead bodies.

She smiled and made her way to the door. "Hi, folks. You're lucky: we have one table left over there," she greeted them, pointing to a corner. "If you want to have a seat either Donna or I will be with you in just a few moments."

The three newcomers made their way to the table, and Denise continued with the coffee on a more expeditious basis. She glanced at the clock as she poured. Thank goodness; they would close in only two more hours…

∞

Ronnie wanted to go out. As a matter of fact, he wanted to go out badly. He knew there was someone out there, someone just waiting for him to find them and… well, make them feel right at home.

But he knew that there were so many police in town right now, so many investigators, and he knew it was him they were wanting to talk to, even if they didn't know it. He curled his fist into a ball as he peeked out the window through a dirty and torn black sheet he had hung over it. It was dark now; maybe he could go without being noticed.

No. That would never work. Something inside him told him he had to wait for all the excitement to die down. Then he would be able to find whoever it was he wanted to look for.

He never knew who they were until he saw them coming, then he recognized them right away. He could tell by the look in their eyes as soon as his met theirs: they couldn't wait for him to show them what he could do. He could see the smiles in their eyes, and the anticipation.

He just couldn't understand why they always had to change their minds right before he was ready to show them exactly what he could do. They would go from friendly and flirty to scared and screaming. The running was frustrating, but the funny thing was it kind of got him ready for... the show.

He stepped away from the window and looked down at his hand. He had been making a hard fist, and he didn't even realize it. His fingernails had carved deep grooves into his palm, and now it was covered in blood. He held his hand up to his nose and closed his eyes, inhaling deeply. His eyes flew open in frustration, and he stuck his tongue out. Then he ran his tongue slowly, languorously even, up the length of his dirty palm, lapping up the blood and dirt that covered it. It tasted heavenly, and he closed his eyes in ecstasy, savoring every second of the metallic flavor as it seemed to caress the inside of his mouth.

Oh, he could hardly wait for all these strangers to go. It was time for them to go! Hadn't they been here long enough already? He needed to taste some blood that wasn't his own.

Now, he made a fist out of the same hand and swung it hard, punching the wall next to the window. The old plaster and drywall crumbled immediately, making him feel powerful and in charge. It calmed and soothed him.

He took a deep breath and squared off his shoulders. Yes, he could wait another day or two if he had to, but he sure hoped all those cops, Darby included, would hurry the hell up. But yes, he would wait.

Now he stepped backwards in the darkness until his back came into contact with the wall. He looked directly down and saw his flashlight on the floor at his feet, right where he had left it when he moved from the kitchen to the living room. The bulb was beginning to weaken and was flickering as it struggled to live. He picked it up and took it back to the kitchen where he opened a drawer filled with packages of tiny flashlight bulbs and batteries. He changed the batteries first, and that did the trick. Now, he smiled and went back to the living room, where he sat down on the floor at his post. From there he could see the headlights of any cars that passed his way, and that would tell him that they were wrapping things up at the ol' murder scene.

He put the lit flashlight on the floor next to him and began to roll it back and forth between his fingers as he fixed his gaze on the tattered black sheet. Beads of sweat formed on his forehead, which he absentmindedly wiped away with his other hand. It was so hot in here all the time; it made him feel crazy.

But with each passing minute, he was closer to the next one, and that was all he was waiting for.

Something inside of him told him to stay put, no matter what. He found himself wishing he had some kind of company to keep his mind off the nagging. As he sat thinking, his head grew heavy, and in a few moments he dropped off to sleep.

∞

Ronald's mother was sitting at the table having her coffee. He came in from outside; he was hungry, and it was very near lunch.

His mother looked at him, surprise and anger all over her face. "What have you been doing, Ronald?"

"Nothin' ma," he replied. "I was just playing in the yard."

"You are bloody and filthy. Where did the blood come from, Dirty Boy?"

Ronnie felt his heart begin to pound, and he was beginning to wonder if what was happening wasn't real. "It's a dream, it's a dream," he was saying over and over, but he couldn't wake himself up.

He looked down to see what his mother was talking about, and he immediately took in a sharp breath: he had blood all over him. Where had it come from? He hadn't hurt any pets, not at this age. He was all of five years old in the dream.

Now, he began to stutter as he turned his hands over and saw the shiny red blood. It had begun to congeal in spots, and he could even see chunks of skin in it. "I-i-I don't know, Mother."

He looked up at her and her face began to change. Her cheekbones sharpened under her skin, and two horns broke through the flesh of her forehead. She cackled at him loudly.

"Dirty boys need a bath!" She walked to the kitchen sink and pulled out the sink cleanser and a chunk of steel wool.

"No! No! I didn't do anything!"

She laughed at him again as she grabbed the whistling teapot from the stove top. "Only hot water will do!"

Now, he crumbled to the floor and put his hands over his head to protect himself. His mother was still laughing, and Ronnie could even hear her footsteps as she drew closer and closer to his cowering body.

"Filthy skin on a bad, bad filthy boy!"

Ronnie screamed.

He jerked awake violently just as his mother had poured the scalding water onto the flesh of his arms. He struggled to come back to reality as he screamed over and over again. Finally, he realized it had been a dream and he broke down in tears.

"Damn, I wish I had a drink," he said into the nothing of his dirty, grimy house. The walls were the only thing that listened to him. Everyone else wanted him to hurt, and it had been that way as long as he could remember.

CHAPTER 10

"Oh My, I think my feet are gonna fall plumb off," Donna said to Denise as she rubbed the arch of her left foot. Her shoes sat on the floor next to the booth, and Denise could smell the sweaty odor, but she said nothing.

They had cleaned up the dining room and done all the necessary side work to prepare for the day tomorrow, and now they were sitting together splitting their tips. It had been an extraordinarily good night. Between the two of them, they had made a hundred and fifty bucks apiece, which was way more than usual. Denise found herself smiling as she tucked the money into her coin purse and dropped it into her apron.

The two of them had half-joked with Dickie about hiring more help for them, but that was all it was: joking. Sure, Diane could use a bit of extra cash during the summer, but she seemed to get by just fine on what she earned helping the locals with yard work and errands. Besides, they didn't typically have enough business for three waitresses, and they both really needed every cent they earned, especially Denise, who was busy with Diane. Donna's kids had grown, and both of them had hit the road long ago.

Denise stood up as Donna put her shoes back on and gathered her own tips to put away. She approached the window just as Dickie put two Styrofoam boxes in the window: Scott's supper.

"Here you go, girlie," he said to her with a smile. "I'm sure your boyfriend is dying for a bite, so you better go on, now, and get it over to him."

Denise gave Dickie a sarcastic grin. "Funny. But you might not be so far off, mister."

"What does that mean?" Dickie got an alarmed look on his face. "You don't need to be foolin' around with no strange men, Denise. You don't know what he's all about now, do you?"

Denise shrugged as she poured a cup of iced tea and capped it, then grabbed a plastic sack for the meal boxes. She also grabbed one of the two cribbage boards and a deck of cards from behind the counter that Dickie kept on hand for the local folk. "I might be finding out what he's all about."

She opened the cooler and grabbed a slice of New York cheesecake she had boxed up earlier. Dickie came through the swinging door that led to the kitchen and leaned his back against the counter. He looked so tired, Denise thought. His hands and arms were covered with burns, and he had dark circles under his eyes. "How's Doris these days, anyway Dickie?"

He shrugged and looked away. "'Bout the same, you know." He scratched behind his ear then met her gaze again. "And don't be changing the subject. I don't think it's safe for you to be fraternizing with strangers."

Denise offered him a smile in an effort to calm him, then she patted him on the shoulder. "Well, he ain't really no stranger now, is he? Besides, we been talking a bit, and he did try to help me, even if he didn't know what was going on."

Donna's sing-song voice came across the room then. "I'm outta here, you two. I feel like my feet have done fell off. I'm ready to go home and try to catch an episode before I doze. Have a good one."

Dickie turned to her and scrunched his face. "How are you gonna watch that garbage when you got the real deal goin' on right here at home?"

Donna just stuck her tongue out and waved goodbye to them both, letting the door swing shut behind her.

"Look Dickie," Denise continued as he turned back to her. "You don't have anything to worry about when it comes to me, okay? That guy ain't interested in hanging out here in Hicksville, and I'm not looking to leave." She rubbed his shoulder reassuringly then turned to pack all the boxes in the bag. She tied a secure knot in the top and checked her apron pocket for the keys to the jail, then grabbed up her things to go.

"Call me when you get home, girlie," he said to her with a wink. "I just wanna be sure you're okay."

She smiled and stood on her tiptoes to kiss his cheek. "I will, and I love you, Dickie. Thank you for all you do, okay?"

He nodded and followed her to the door, which he locked as soon as she went out. He reached up and flipped off the dining room light just as the phone pealed with its loud ringing. Dickie crossed the room and grabbed the receiver from its cradle on the wall.

"Dickie's."

Sheriff Darby's voice came over the line. "Hey, Dick. How's tricks?"

It was a greeting he usually used in good cheer, but his voice gave his true mood away. The sheriff sounded exhausted and frustrated. Dickie's eyes squinted as he spoke cautiously, trying to read the cop's mood.

"Oh, all's well, I s'pose," he replied. "We got slammed in here today, for sure. The press and tourists 'bout ate me outta business."

"Ayuh, I expected," Darby replied. "Are the girls still there?"

Dickie leaned back against the counter, a common resting place for both him and the girls. "Nope. Donna's gone, and Denise just left to take your boy his supper. Sorry we got it out late; we were just too busy."

"No problem." Darby reassured him. "That was what I wanted to talk to you about anyway."

Now Dickie's antennas went up. They always did when the sheriff wanted to 'talk' to him. It seemed like every time the topic was something that made him worry, though he didn't always know why. "What's up, Bobby?"

Darby took a deep, audible breath on the other end of the phone. "I guess I been worrying about that inmate. You don't think it's... dangerous to be letting Denise take him food, do you?"

Dickie was quiet for a moment. He scratched his chin as he thought. He had been living in Burdensville way too long, and he felt like he knew too much. He had toyed with the idea of gathering up Doris and moving to the city, but he knew deep in his heart he was trapped here, partially because of his roots and partially because... well, he was trapped.

"Look, Bobby, it wasn't a good idea for you to take the guy in, to begin with," Dickie replied. "It would have taken attention off the situation if you had just packed up Ronnie, but you and your hard headed sense of misplaced obligation, you know?"

Darby cleared his throat. "Dickie, I didn't ask for your opinion about my personal life. I have reasons for the things I choose to do, and I keep everyone's best interest in mind all the time." He was getting agitated, but so was Dickie with the entire confusing situation. "Just answer the question, please. I'm tired, and I just wanna know what you think."

"Denise could be trusted with my life, and yours, for that matter," Dickie said, not hiding his own frustration. "You should have thought about that more clearly before you recruited her. I didn't like to put her in that position to begin with."

"Well," Darby said, lightly now. "That was all I needed, friend. I have to travel to the state police office in the morning with some paperwork on recent incidents, you know, photos and the like. The next day, I have some yard work to do for Ronnie that I promised him. His lawn is overgrown. If you feel okay about Denise, well, I'd appreciate her help for the next day or two. If you're uncomfortable, well…"

Now Dickie shook his head to himself; damn Darby. "You know I can't do it myself, especially with the way business is going due to all this commotion. She'll do it, but if I were you, I'd offer her a bit of a reward when you can. She's handling your damn dirty work and doesn't even know it."

"Fine, fine, Dickie," Darby continued, as if he hadn't even heard him. "Thanks for all your help, and I'll give you a ring tomorrow."

The phone went dead, and Dickie stared at the receiver. "That so-and-so rear end, Darby." He hung it up and went into the kitchen, where he shut things down and turned off the lights. Darby had a way of using people for his own ends, and Dickie knew it. It made him sick, but what could he do?

He locked up the café and started the short walk home. He would make it a point of going by the jail just to peek in the window at Denise and the prisoner before he went home to Doris. He hoped she had remembered to take her medicine; it seemed like lately her mind was going out the door right along with her ability to breathe.

Dickie trudged along up the narrow sidewalk, his back aching and his feet throbbing.

R.W.K. Clark

CHAPTER 11

"So, you were really married before?" Denise was sitting in the folding chair outside of Scott's cell, while he sat on his cot tearing into his chicken fried steak as though he were starving to death. She was eager to take him on in a game of cribbage, but he needed to eat first. She did have the board and cards ready to go, however.

He wiped his mouth with his napkin, then swallowed. "Yes, briefly." His voice had a bit of a drag to it, and Denise could sense his grief.

"What happened?" she asked. "I mean, you don't have to tell me if you don't want to, obviously." She laughed nervously and began that picking at her apron that she habitually did.

Scott shook his head and took a drink of his tea. "I don't mind," he replied. "I mean, even last week I might not have wanted to talk about it, but you have a way of making me comfortable."

Denise looked up at him then, the blood rising to her cheeks. She smiled shyly, then sat on her hands and looked at him expectantly. Scott sat back and crossed his hands over his chest. He took a deep breath.

"Breast cancer," he said. "It ran in her family. We were married for only two years, but we were together longer."

Denise sucked in a breath and then tried to compose herself. She was sure he was tired of those shocked reactions; she knew she was when people asked about her parents, which didn't happen so often anymore. It could be overwhelming.

"I'm so sorry, Scott."

He shook his head and began to stir his mashed potatoes around with his plastic fork. "Don't be. I'm finally starting to get over it. That's the reason I started this 'traveling', you know. I had to work my way through the pain somehow, and I guess, I thought that going from town to town was the equivalent of running away."

Denise nodded her head in agreement. "I would have to say that is exactly what it is. Has it helped?"

"Well," he continued, "I thought I would lose my mind with missing her after it was all over. It was like there was a big empty spot everywhere in my life, and there was nothing that was ever going to fill it, ever again. When she died, my sense of home died with her, so I just up and left."

Denise nodded once again, this time with understanding. "I know just the feeling you're talking about. If it wasn't for my sister, I think, I would have felt the exact same way, but she gave me a reason to… live. A reason to stay. She was 'home'."

"The truth is that, up until now, the running hasn't helped a bit," he answered her question. "The fact is, it seemed to make it worse and worse."

Scott smiled and took another bite of his food. It was actually very exhilarating to talk to someone, anyone, about Kelly. Especially when he was able to feel like someone got it. What a relief to know that, no matter how he had been feeling since she passed, someone on Earth really could relate.

He put his fork down. "Denise, I know you know why the sheriff acted the way he did, and I also know you are holding back. What's going on with him and Ronnie?"

Denise stood and began to pace nervously. She looked around as if someone were hiding in the shadows listening to what they were saying. When she seemed satisfied that they were alone, she came up close to the bars of the cell. "Sheriff Darby has always sort of taken Ronnie under his wing, like I said."

"Why?" He stood as well and stood across from her, his hands curling around the bars.

Denise shrugged and let her eyes flitter here and there. "I don't know, really. It's been like that as long as I can remember. I know that Ronnie's parents are dead, and so are the sheriff's. Maybe he feels obligated because of it."

"So he arrests strangers?"

She laughed lightly. "No, silly," she said. "Actually, that's the first time that I know of that he has ever done anything like that. I think everyone was a bit surprised, but we all know how he feels about him, so no one wanted to piss him off anymore, you know?"

Scott stared at her for a minute, then said, "No, I don't know."

"In your situation, and knowing Darby like I do, I feel safe saying that I think it angered him that some 'stranger' would come into town and presume to know Ronnie," she said. "I'm sure that's all it was."

Now Scott started to pace around his cell, his food forgotten. He was going to tread lightly here; it was not his place to presume. She was right about that, and that was precisely what he had done. Now was a good time to change the subject.

"Do you think you'll be bringing me my breakfast?"

Denise smiled at him and blushed once again. "I don't know; we hadn't heard from Darby when I left the café. Why?"

"Well," Scott replied. "Don't go out of your way, especially if Darby is bringing it, but if you do, would you mind bringing me the paper? I sure would like something to read."

Denise flashed him a big grin and turned around. She walked to a small row of three institutional-looking padded chairs next to the main door. On top of the first one sat a pile of rolled up newspapers. She grabbed them all and came back to him. "I'll still bring you tomorrow's edition if I come, but these should tide you over until then."

Now it was Scott's turn to smile, and he flashed her one of his best. "You're amazing!"

She giggled like a schoolgirl and shook her head, then she continued. "I'll even leave the lights on, the ones back near you. That way you can read, okay?"

She shoved the papers through the bars one at a time. There were six in all, which told Scott the sheriff hadn't been reading them. Actually, he likely got them at home and read them in the morning with his coffee, Scott thought. That made more sense.

"Well," she said. "I should be going, I guess. If Diane's still up, she may be worried. Maybe I'll see you tomorrow?"

Scott threw the papers onto his bunk and grabbed onto the bars again, putting his face between two of them as far as it would go. "I really hope so," he said. "Hey, what about our game?"

∞

The two spent the next half hour playing cribbage. They both laughed more than they could remember, and they found each other's company mutually enjoyable. Denise finally looked at her watch.

"It's getting pretty late, Scott. I'm pretty tired."

"Me too," he said as she shifted her weight from one foot to the other and crossed her arms over her chest. Then she looked him in the eye, then quickly looked away. It tickled him the way she was so nervous around him. He wondered what it would be like to kiss her good.

Suddenly, Denise leaned forward and kissed him square on the lips. It wasn't quite what he had been fantasizing about, but it sent a jolt of electricity up his spine nonetheless. She pulled away, and waved her hand at him, then abruptly turned and left, shutting the door quickly and locking it behind her.

Scott stared at the door in shock. Slowly a smile came over his face, and he got a dreamy look in his eye. She hadn't even remembered to turn off the lights at the front. He sat down on the foot of his cot and kicked his feet back and forth like a teenager. She was certainly something special.

After a full ten minutes, he stood up and gathered the food he had not eaten, putting it in one box. He found the cheesecake then; she had actually tried to surprise him, and it worked. He used his fingers to eat it, dropping graham cracker crumbs down his front as he wolfed it down. Then he gulped the rest of his tea and put the remainder of his food aside to snack on later, if he wanted.

He sat cross-legged on the bed and sorted the papers out by date. They went back five days, and then there was one for that day. He started with the oldest, taking the rubber band off and snapping it across the room. It consisted of a total of four pages only. It would take him no time to read it.

The paper consisted mostly of local updates for the high school. There were also some stories on what local committees were doing, as well as a piece on a pile of quilts that a pair of twins from town had made and donated to a cancer hospice in the City.

State sports, weather, and county obituaries were in the following pages. He was almost through completely when he saw a tiny piece on the very last page consisting of only two small paragraphs:

Young Woman Found Murdered Outside of Burdensville

The story told only of a young woman's body found in a ditch about two miles outside of town. She had been raped, and her larynx had been crushed. A 2001 Beetle with a flat had been deserted, and while the owner of the car had been traced, the article did not specify whether or not it belonged to the woman. Her identity would not be released pending notification of kin.

The last paragraph mentioned very briefly that the murder was the latest in a string, and the killer had not yet been captured. The paper went on to warn residents to avoid travel on roads just outside of Burdensville until the capture of the 'offender'. It ended there.

Now, Scott's interest was piqued, and he opened the next paper eagerly. He was disappointed, though; neither of the following three papers contained any kind of continuance or update regarding the murder. He safely assumed that the state police had not gotten involved in that investigation.

Finally he opened the last one, but he had no high hopes about what he would find. He was surprised when he opened it and the front page blared:

State Police Investigate Latest Burdensville Murders:

Two Found Dead Outside Burdensville; State Police Say the Line Must Be Drawn on Negligent and Faulty Investigative Tactics

State Police have intervened in the investigation into two murders which were just discovered outside Burdensville. The murders are only the latest in a string of unsolved murders which have taken place on the outskirts of town. Initially, Sheriff Robert Darby of Burdensville was handling all investigations, which were being conducted by him exclusively, but according to Mary Kay Monroe, spokeswoman for the State Police and Bureau of Investigation, state officials have stepped in due to what they are referring to as 'gross negligence' on the part of Sheriff Darby.

At the current time, there are a total of five murders which have taken place just outside of town. The first body was discovered two months ago at the abandoned Wilson farm by three local junior high school students. The body was that of Katie Castleman, 19, of Handom. Castleman was a student at the State College, and according to family, had been on her way to visit friends in Rumming. It was reported to this paper that

Castleman had been driving a 2000 Taurus, but the vehicle was never recovered.

The second victim was murdered and discovered one month ago. She was identified as Jane Feister, 21, of Greenville. Feister's body was discovered along Highway 16 by a passing motorist. She was partially clothed and severely beaten. Feister's family reported that the woman had been driving a 1990 Prelude, but as in the first case, a vehicle was never found.

Victim number three was Carly Reed, 23, of Fester. Ms. Reed had been traveling to an interview for a teaching position, but reportedly never made it. Her body was found by Burdensville locals, who wish to remain anonymous. Her vehicle, a 2001 Beetle, was also discovered approximately eight miles away from where her body was found.

The most recent victims, which the State Police are currently investigating after interjecting in Sheriff Darby's investigation, were Timothy Bascom, 18, and Meredith Downs, 17, of Rumming. The two teens were reportedly driving to attend a rock and roll concert in the City. Bascom was discovered with fatal head trauma alongside Highway 16. Miss Downs was discovered in a nearby field. The vehicle they were driving was parked on the highway about fifty feet from Bascom's body.

All the victims, with the exception of Bascom, had been sexually violated and severely beaten. Three of them showed signs of their throats being crushed. No other details regarding the victims have been reported at the current time.

Sheriff Darby is being interviewed by State Police, with a variety of serious questions being posed as to why the sheriff did not request assistance from them at any point. There are also accusations that an abundance of evidence may have either been ignored or overlooked during the investigations he conducted.

We will report any further updates on the case as they are received.

Scott looked up from the paper, his heart beating fast. He couldn't believe what he had just read. A town the size of Burdensville, that had fallen victim to such violence, should have been swarming with state police when it all began. How did Darby manage to sweep all this crap under the rug the way he had? Someone had to be helping him and covering for him somehow.

Now, Scott began to flip through the few remaining pages of the paper, paying special attention to the box ads that took up most of the page space. There was an announcement for the Burdensville K-12 school and a fundraiser they were having; this let him know that the small town had its own educational system, but that wasn't what he was looking for. There was also an ad for a dentist named Dr. Jethro Means, who did general dental care. Finally, in the lower right hand corner of the last page, he found what he had been seeking, and his eyes lit up.

It was a box ad for the Burdensville Medical Center, and the ad was smaller than all the rest on the page. The head doctor, and from the looks of it the only doctor at the center, was Dr. Ivan Smith. It stated that Dr. Smith was the town's only physician, and he ran the center as a family practice. It specified that Dr. Smith gave referrals for major care as needed and was a lifelong resident of Burdensville. "Dr. Smith is your friend in medicine!" the ad boldly stated, and next to that there was a yellow smiley face.

Now Scott stood up and began to pace in the small confines of his cell. Sweat was trickling down his armpits, and he was aware of the odor that was emanating from them. He wanted to get out of this cell, and badly. If three murders had taken place without the knowledge or investigative assistance of the State Police, then someone had to take care of the bodies, someone had to have contacted the next of kin and either done the autopsies or prepared them for transport.

Had it been Ivan Smith?

He plopped down on his cot and put his head in his hands. Surely the police were going to check into this. Surely they were going to narrow down how the murders had managed to slip by everyone's attention or concern. Surely they were going to be asking all the right questions.

He cleared the papers from his bed and lay down. He found he could hardly wait for the paper the next morning, if Denise was the one to bring his breakfast anyway. From the way it sounded, Darby was going to have his hands full for a bit trying to clear his name, so Denise was exactly who Scott expected to see.

CHAPTER 12

Darby steered his patrol car down Highway 16, the radio off and his finger tapping the steering wheel nervously. He would be home in around twenty minutes, but the first stop he was going to make was not his home. No, he needed to deal with the mess that had been made, and a great big damn mess it was, too.

Sure, the State Police had told him to go ahead and get back to Burdensville; after all, he was the only cop the town had. They wanted him back bright and early in the morning, though. They were far from done with their fishing and their questions, and his stomach roiled nervously at the thought.

He needed to talk to Ivan, but, most of all, he needed to have words with Ronnie... some very, very serious words.

He found himself fretting over what had been going on, but not for the lives of the girls, which had been taken so violently from them. No, he fretted for what he considered to be his failure. He had failed Ronnie.

As he drove, Darby let his mind wander back to the past, to the very beginning of it all. That had been when he truly got off course, when it came to his sense of obligation to the man the town knew as Ronnie Smith.

∞

Bobby's mother had been growing. At least, that was how he saw it. Her belly had been getting bigger and bigger. Bobby thought she was beautiful, but his Daddy hated it. He called her 'pig' and 'fat pig', and sometimes, when he had the soda pop in the white and red can, he would even hit her just for getting fatter.

He would hit her in the belly or the face. She would hardly make a sound, but tears would come out of her eyes. She would go about her business of taking care of Bobby and Daddy, but sometimes after she got hit, it would be harder for her to move around than ever.

One day, right after Mommy put some spaghetti in front of him, his daddy came home early from his job. When he saw that all mommy had made was the canned pasta, he got really mad. "This is why you're such a fat pig, you pig!" He hit her in the belly with his fist, and Mommy had fallen on the floor.

She had blood coming out of her then; it was on the hem and the back of her dress, and she started to really holler and cry. She was saying 'It hurts!', and she acted like she couldn't breathe. Bobby had left his bowl of spaghetti at the table and was crouched in a corner of the kitchen, shaking. Daddy paced around while blood came out of his mother. "What do you want me to do? I suppose, you want me to call Doc, but I ain't doin' it!" His father looked worried, pacing around like he was trying to figure out what to do. "Doc has his own problems, you know. His missus just lost a kid herself, and I ain't goin' ta jail on account of you!"

The pain had gotten worse for his mom, he could tell, and finally she had splayed her legs out and started to act like she had to poop. Bobby covered his eyes, and when he opened them his daddy was on the floor between his mom's legs. "Bobby, go get me a towel or a sheet or something'!" Bobby jumped up and ripped his own blanket off his bed and ran it to his dad. When he got there, his daddy was holding a slippery little person with blood all over it. It was crying and screaming, but his mommy was just lying there. She wasn't crying, but she was sure bleeding all over.

"Mommy needs a Band-aid, Daddy," Bobby had said, but his daddy didn't care; he was too busy wrapping that baby up in the blanket. Bobby bent over his mommy. Her eyes were open a little, and she was sure white and sweaty. "Do you need some Band-aids, Mommy?"

Mommy smiled a little bit, but not very much. "Mommy's goin' away now," she said. She was only whispering, and Bobby had to get really close to her face to hear her. "Where you goin', Mommy?" She didn't answer his question, though. She just kept on whispering. "No matter what you take care of him, okay? You take care of that baby…"

Those were the last words Bobby's mommy ever said to him, and they never left him, never gave him any relief.

∞

Darby shook his head violently, shaking the memories from it, and along with them, the pain. He slowed the car as it approached the gravel road he was looking for; it was dark, but he knew Burdensville and all of its outskirts like the back of his hand. Sure enough, the darkened road came into the headlights, and Darby swung a left.

He was only a few miles from Ronnie's now, the home that had been his when he was a boy. Even in the darkness, he could recognize every tree and fencepost. It made his mind wander once again...

∞

Mommy did go away that day; she went to Heaven, and Bobby never saw her again.

Daddy had called Doc Smith, and he came over to the house. "I don't know what I'ma gonna do, Doc. Ain't no one gonna believe I didn't cause this... no one."

Doc Smith had covered his Mommy with a sheet and sat at the table with Daddy. Bobby was supposed to be in his bed, but he had hidden around the corner in the hallway and watched and listened to the men. For a long time, Doc had sat with his head in his hands while Daddy held a bottle in the baby's mouth, I can't do this! I can't handle a little baby. Finally, Doc looked up and said, "I have a solution, and it's the only one I can think of." They talked about Doc Smith taking the new baby to his house to live. Since his own had just been stillborn, and he hadn't told anyone per his wife's request, they could take the child as his own, and his wife would help tend to the baby. He would make up the right papers that would say Bobby's mommy died having the new baby, and the baby died as well.

Bobby didn't understand all they were saying, but it sounded to him like they were going to tell lies. Bobby got a spanking if he told lies, and he didn't understand why it was okay for grown-ups to tell lies.

The doctor took the baby, and then his daddy started for the hallway. Bobby had run to his room like lightning, but his daddy knew he'd been sneaking. "I ain't gonna beat you boy; I've screwed up enough for one day." His daddy looked worn out and beaten up, sort of. "Now, I heard what your momma told you. That boy is goin' to live with Doc and his wife; they'll be his ma and pa. But you, you will always be his brother. Your ma was right; you need to take care of him, no matter what. You got it?" Bobby had nodded, and without another word his daddy left the room.

∞

About a half-mile up, Darby saw the single light that stood high over that old house where all those things had taken place. It was Ronnie's house now; his brother Ronnie. It was broken down and overgrown (he suddenly remembered he needed to mow the yard that coming weekend), but it was a safe place for the messed up man to live.

He finally reached the drive and took another left. He pulled up the dirt drive slowly, his eyes peeled in the darkness as he tried to see any movement or lights in the windows. There was nothing though. All was still, and very, very quiet.

He turned off the ignition and heaved his large body from the driver's seat. He then reached into the passenger side and retrieved his big, heavy Mag-Lite. Darby turned it on and aimed it at the front of the house. That was when he saw one of the window coverings twitch a bit. Yep, Ronnie was inside, and he was awake. He was likely waiting for Darby to come and give him the talking that he knew he was in for.

The sheriff made his way around to the door in the back, the one that led to the kitchen. It was slightly ajar when he reached it, telling him that Ronnie had opened it for him and then went back into the house to hide. He entered, then turned around and secured the door behind him.

"Ronnie, you need to come on out here now, ayuh," Darby hollered. He could be anywhere in the house, and Darby wasn't about to engage in a game of hide and seek like he had done with him so many times before. "Now I ain't playin', Ronnie. If I gotta come look for you, we're gonna have us a bit of a brawl."

He saw the man's shadow slowly creep around the corner of the living room and come into the kitchen.

Darby shined his light at the shadow and there Ronnie stood, his own flashlight turned off and held in an iron grip in his hands. He was dirty, and there was a slight shy smile on his lips.

"How you doin', Bobby?"

Darby shifted his weight from one foot to the other and focused on maintaining a stern look. "Not so damn good, Ronnie. Not good."

"Whassa matter?"

Now Darby felt fury. Ronnie knew what the matter was. He was so much like a damn kid, and sometimes it was just too much of a burden for the single small-town sheriff to bear.

"We've talked about this before," he began, "And I've told you what could happen if you kept up your crap, hurting these girls, killin' and rapin' but you didn't wanna listen, and now the crap's fixin' to hit the fan, boy."

Ronnie started to tremble, but he took a step toward Darby anyway. A wave of alcoholic reek hit the sheriff in the face like a brick wall, and in the stream coming from the flashlight, he could see blood running down Ronnie's arm.

"You been hurtin' yourself, again?" he asked.

Ronnie looked down and didn't answer.

"Well, I'm just gonna lay it out: they're fixin' to have my job, and my rear, over the covering I been doing for you," he said. "They're on to us now but good, and I don't even know if I can do anything about it."

Ronnie looked up at him, his eyes frightened. "You'll fix it, Bobby. You always fix it. I didn't mean any harm. Them girls, they liked it. They liked me!"

Darby took three steps forward and slapped the man hard across the face. Ronnie staggered as his hand went to his cheek. "No! No, they didn't like it! You been killing! You sick pain in my butt! You're takin' their lives!"

Ronnie began to cry then, and Darby felt a lurch of nausea. "Look, Ronnie, I'm sorry I hit you." He reached up and took the man in his arms and pulled him to him. He held him and let him cry it out. Oh, ma, he thought as he rubbed Ronnie's back. "I can't do this. I don't think I can take care of him anymore."

After the man's sobs subsided, Darby stood him at arm's length and shone his flashlight on his chest just enough to get a look at his face. He pulled a handkerchief out of his brown trousers and handed it over. "Blow your nose," he said gruffly, and Ronnie obeyed.

"Now, I need you to listen to me close, and I need you to do what I tell you, no matter what."

Ronnie nodded as he wiped at his nose and sniffled.

"No drinking, Ronnie. That's the most important thing," Darby said, shaking a finger at the man. "None of this crap even started until you started sucking on that damn bottle day in and day out. No drinking."

Ronnie looked panicked and stricken, but he only nodded. "Next, I want you to stay here. No leaving, no going to town, not for anything. Where's the keys to your car?"

Ronnie took a step back. "No, Bobby. Don't take Old Mabel. Not my car."

"What are you gonna need it for if you're doing what I tell you to do?" He was starting to raise his voice again. He needed Ronnie to understand that he had to do everything he was telling him to do. There could be no deviation, none whatsoever.

Ronnie squared off his shoulders a bit and shoved the hanky in his front pocket. "What if there's an emergency, and you're not around, huh? I ain't got no phone, and there ain't no neighbors nearby. What then, huh?"

Darby considered his words for a bit. He was right; he didn't have any way to get ahold of anyone if something did happen. That was why he gave him the car in the first place. "Okay. But there ain't gonna be no drinking, and no driving unless you just gotta, understand?"

Ronnie nodded again, a huge look of relief on his face. Darby continued, "I'm gonna be dealing with the State for the next day or two. This weekend, I'm gonna come and help you with the yard and such. Do you have enough food to get you by for a day or two?"

Ronnie looked thoughtful for a moment. "I have some chips, and a few cans of spaghetti, and I got my can opener! I've got some soda in the can."

"Okay," Darby replied, satisfied. "That'll do you for a couple of days. I'm hoping to be gone only tomorrow, but at this point, I still don't know what's gonna happen, Ronnie. That's why it's so important for you to lay low. We don't want anyone to suspect it's been you that's done anything."

"Do they now?" Ronnie's voice was low, and he sounded scared once again.

Darby shook his head. "Naw, I don't think so. But if they start asking questions around town, I can't guarantee that no one will talk about you and me, and about the way you act, Ronnie. That's why you gotta lay low, so you'll pass from their minds, you see."

Ronnie let out a loud sigh. "Okay, Bobby. I'll do what you say."

Now Darby gave another nod, one of completion. He patted Ronnie on the shoulder. "So I'm gonna go now. Are you gonna be okay here?"

"Ayuh," Ronnie replied. "Wouldn't wanna be anywhere else, Bobby."

Darby left then and aimed his car up the gravel road toward town. As he drove, he thought some more about the situation. He felt like it was suffocating him.

∞

He spent his life looking out for that kid. It had been obvious from the start that something just wasn't right with Ronnie Smith. He didn't learn like other kids in school, and right after first grade, Doc Smith had taken him out of public education and Mrs. Smith had started to teach him from home. Bobby would visit about three days a week and play with him, but Ronnie never had any idea the boy was his own brother, his own flesh and blood.

"You don't ever tell no one about it, you hear me boy?" His father had drilled it into him from the start. He was to remain in Ronnie's life, be there for him and have his back, but no one was to know they were kin. This was to protect his dad from what had been done to his mother, and protect Doc Smith from what he had done to cover the whole thing up. "Someday I'm gonna be gone, and so are the Smiths. The only one Ronnie is gonna have is you, so I expect you to mind that carefully."

Robert Darby had done just that.

After a couple of years, Doc and Mrs. Smith had another child, another boy. They called him Ivan as well, and Ivan was the apple of his parents' eyes. He excelled in all he did: he was at the top of his class; he participated in, and ran, all the sports he could. He was good looking, and he wanted to be a doctor, just like his father. It wasn't long after his birth that Ronnie started to fade into the background of the perfect family 'photo'. He was the idiot, the embarrassment. Ivan was favored, and it showed.

Robert saw it, and he despised the Smiths for it, but there was nothing he could do. As the boys all grew into their teen years, things became increasingly worse for Ronnie. He would wander around town on his yellow bike with the banana seat, and the neighbors would give him change and candy. Everyone knew that Ronnie Smith was the 'boy his parents didn't want'.

Robert had started to hang out down at the police station, and the sheriff then, Mac Ludwig, had become his mentor. Robert's father had taken ill and was put in a home with alcoholic dementia at a pretty young age. He died of liver cancer there, and he left Robert the house, but Robert stayed with Sheriff Ludwig, who eventually got him into the police academy. He was being groomed to take over as the sheriff of Burdensville.

Ivan Smith went off to college and studied medicine; he would take over his father's family practice at Burdensville Clinic, now known as Burdensville Medical Center. Ronnie stayed in Burdensville, lonely, unloved, and confused. He rode his bike around town and entertained himself the best he could.

While Robert was gone away at the Academy, Ronnie had a spot of trouble. Ludwig had been called by a number of locals to deal with their pets and livestock being found brutally killed. At first, Ludwig had thought it was teenaged toughs terrorizing the townsfolk from one of the bigger cities, kids just trying to get their kicks, but one day, right before graduation, Robert got a call from Ludwig.

"Ronnie was caught slicing up one of the old twins' cats. He was inflicting the same damage that's been done to all the other animals in town."

Bobby asked him, "Are you gonna lock him up?"

Ludwig replied, "Naw, I just can't do it. Mrs. Smith's had a stroke, and Doc ain't too well himself. We promised the folks it would stop, but we just don't know what to do with him."

Robert had gone to bed that night with the weight of the world on his shoulders. He had cried with his face in his pillow, begging his deceased mother to forgive him for leaving Ronnie and going off to the Academy. That was when he thought about the house.

It hadn't been cared for in a while, but he could take an early graduation and go home and clean the place up. He had all his credits, after all, and would be interning with Ludwig. Then Ronnie could have the house; he could go live on the outskirts of Burdensville, where he wouldn't hurt the animals or scare the townsfolk.

It was the perfect solution...

∞

Now Darby was pulling into town in his cruiser. Finally; he was so damned tired and hungry that he could hardly stand it, and he wanted a hot shower.

The town was peaceful and picturesque. Not a soul stirred, and Darby felt a rush of love and affection for Burdensville that he hadn't felt in a very long time. He had to figure things out, had to fix things. He had no idea what to do about Ronnie, but there had to be a solution.

He got to his house and went quickly inside. There he ate a microwave dinner while he watched the news on the small TV set in his kitchen. He then took a steaming shower and made his way to bed.

He was glad to be home, but even in his exhaustion, sleep evaded him. He was in real trouble here, and he knew it. Best case scenario was him being forced to resign. At the worst, he was going to do some time. The thought made him ill.

CHAPTER 13

Scott woke early in his jail cell, while the sun was still hiding from the sky. He had read, and reread the papers Denise had let him have the evening before, and he found that he had more questions building up in his mind than a passing-through stranger had a right to have. He could hardly wait for her to arrive, because some of them were for her.

He washed himself as best he could in the small stainless-steel sink. He could smell himself, and when he thought about their brief kiss the night before, he became worried that she had as well. If she did, she hadn't let on to the fact, so all he could do was hope that she was none the wiser.

By sunrise, he was very antsy indeed. He entertained himself for a while by playing Solitaire with the cards Denise had brought; then, he played himself in Cribbage a couple of times. He had thought about doing a crossword but he didn't even have a pencil that he could use. The cards would have to do. He did some push-ups and sit-ups. He made his bed and straightened his cell.

Finally, at seven, he lay back down on his cot and tried to refocus his thoughts until his food came.

It was all he could do to not stare at the knob of the jail door.

Denise Jensen was a surprise. Scott had convinced himself that he would never be interested in another female, yet here he was in a small town jail cell, and he couldn't get the little waitress off his mind. His brain wanted to play tricks on him and tell him he was horrible, that he was betraying his precious Kelly, but his heart knew better. Trying to buck up and move on was likely the very best thing for him.

She was cute and funny and smart and independent. He found himself wanting to know everything about her. He also found himself wishing he could take care of her and protect her, and he hadn't felt that way in a very long time. The fact was, when Kelly died a bit of his sense of manhood died with her. If he couldn't protect her, who could he protect? Was he even a man at all?

Scott was smart; he knew the thoughts he had toward himself regarding Kelly's death were unfair, but he was afraid if he wasn't hard on himself, he may forget, and then it could happen again. No, he wanted to run and hide from life. The funny thing was that the way he felt about Denise so far wasn't going to let him continue to do that. He couldn't even imagine leaving the forsaken town of Burdensville if it meant leaving the little waitress behind.

He lay back down on his cot, trying to force himself to be patient, but it didn't work too well. Before he knew it, he was going through the personal entertainment cycle again: cards, exercise, pace, lie down. It was driving him nuts having to wait like this.

She would be here soon, and he would survive until then.

∞

"Denise, I wonder if you could come in a bit early today," Dickie was saying into the phone. "Sheriff Darby already left for his business, and he needs us to take care of that guy down at the jail."

Denise was still in her pajamas and robe. Diane was in the shower getting ready for school. Even with the morning being so crammed, she found herself more than excited at the thought of seeing Scott Sharp once again.

"Absolutely, Dickie," she replied. "Diane will be out of the bathroom in a bit, I'll get a quick shower, and then I'll be right down to the café. Will that do?"

Dickie looked at the clock on his kitchen wall. It was six-thirty; Darby had called him at six. The café didn't technically open until eight, but he had already taken care of Doris and made sure she had eaten and had her medicine. She was watching TV, so that timetable would work out just fine for him.

"Sounds good, honey. So I'll see you down there by seven-thirty?" he asked.

Denise smiled into the phone; Dickie sounded anxious. "How about seven-fifteen, at the latest."

"Aw, girl, I love you like one of my own." He hung up the phone and went in to kiss Doris. "I'll be home tonight; not sure what time, what with all the rigmarole, but the neighbor will be here to bring you your lunch and your midday remedies, okay lover?"

Doris nodded and he bent over and kissed her warmly. Then he put on his jacket and went out into the cool of the day. The sun was up and the birds were singing. It would be a good day, even if they were as slammed as yesterday.

By the time he opened the café and got the grill heated up and the coffee going, Denise walked in, flushed with good health and smiling. "How'd you sleep, Dick?"

"As good as possible, ayuh," he said, returning her grin. He cracked a couple of eggs on the griddle and laid out a package of bacon. "I'll have breakfast ready for Darby's inmate shortly. Go ahead and get the extras bagged up for him. I don't know what today's gonna be like, so I want you to get back as soon as possible."

Denise quickly poured a cup of milk and one of coffee, then lidded up both of them. Dickie had Scott's breakfast done quickly and put it in the window. "Here you go," he said to her as she opened up a plastic bag to put the food in. "I'll see you shortly."

Dickie turned back to the kitchen, and Denise got the food bagged up and headed out the door, bag on her arm and a cup in both hands. The morning was a little cool, but the sun was shining brightly. She put her face up to the sun and inhaled deeply. It was going to be a beautiful day.

∞

In less than five minutes she was at the jail. She had sort of expected the sheriff to be there, just to check on his inmate before he left town to deal with the state police, but there were no cars at all in front of the building. She put the cups down on the railing of the front porch and dug the keys out of her pocket. Soon, she was inside smiling at Scott, who was up and standing at the bars.

"Good morning," she said cheerfully. "How did you sleep?"

Scott smiled, happy to see her. "Not so good, to be honest. You're a sight for sore eyes, though. I was beginning to think you would never come."

"Well, here I am," she replied. "And here is your breakfast. I'll just grab the morning paper too."

Denise gave him the food and drink items, then went back to the door to fetch the morning paper from the front porch. "What kept you from sleeping?" she asked him over her shoulder.

"I read the papers you gave me last night," he began. "Do you read the paper?"

Denise came back to his cell with the rolled up newspaper and handed it to him through the bars. "No, I really don't. I don't watch much television, either. I guess you read something that occupied your thoughts."

Scott nodded at her. "It seems the state police are investigating Darby for negligence on these murders that have been happening around here."

Denise's mouth dropped open a bit and she raised her eyebrows. "Really? That's why he has to go to the headquarters, huh?"

"Looks that way," he said. He took the lid off his coffee and took a drink, then set it down and took the rubber band from the paper she had just handed him.

"The whole town is talking about it, but I have a hard time believing he'd get in much trouble," she continued. "He's only trying to look after Ronnie; he has always looked after Ronnie."

Scott took another drink of his coffee. "There is something that bothers me."

"What's that?"

"Well," Scott said, "The papers listed all the recent murder victims, and now Darby is being questioned for covering them up or whatever. How did he do that so well? I mean, he would have had to have help from someone to deal with the corpses. You know what I mean?"

Now Denise nodded, a faraway look in her eyes. "It would have to be a doctor that helped him with that; it would be the only way."

"Maybe Dr. Ivan Smith?" Scott asked.

Denise met his gaze. "Dr. Smith is good friends with Darby. He would be the only one I can think of that would do such a thing."

Scott unrolled the paper and laid it flat on his cot. The headline blared out at him:

Investigators Believe Murderer is Local.

State Police Continue to Question Burdensville Sheriff.

Police will continue their line of questioning in regard to the recent murders in the Burdensville area and Sheriff Robert Darby. While investigators have not revealed what they suspect Darby has done, they have released information that they are convinced the murders were committed by someone local to Burdensville.

Darby is expected to undergo interrogation throughout the day today, and perhaps even into tomorrow. The press has been unable to get a statement from the sheriff himself, who has stated that he had no comment pending the closure of the state police investigation as far as it involves him.

The spokesperson for the police has stated that they will begin questioning town locals on an extended basis when they are finished with the line of questioning they are carrying out with Sheriff Darby. These interviews may begin as early as Monday morning.

If anyone has any information or has seen anything at all relating to the murders, they are encouraged to contact the State Police.

The article was brief and offered no further details, but even as Scott read it aloud to Denise, he had a feeling that things were crashing down in the small town of Burdensville. He looked up at her to assess the look on her face, but her stare was blank. He didn't want to upset her with his thoughts, but he had a feeling she was thinking the same thing he was, or maybe she already knew what he thought he knew. After all, Burdensville was her life-long home.

"Denise," he began slowly, "I know I'm not from here, and I don't know anyone that lives here, but I have my own suspicions."

Denise stood. "I really can't stay. Dickie thinks we're gonna have another rush again. I'll bring your lunch, but it might be a bit late."

"Denise, I know you know what I'm thinking," Scott persisted.

Now, she looked him right in the eye, and Scott thought he detected tears pooling slightly in her eyes. "So what do you think, Scott?"

"I think, there is more to Ronnie Smith than meets the eye," he said. "And I think, you know that."

Her hand went up and she brushed away a single tear. "Look," she began, "I have lived here my entire life. I have my younger sister going off to college, and I have a peaceful existence. I'm not a cop, and I don't want to second-guess someone I have known since I was born."

Scott stood and approached the bars of the cell, weighing his words carefully so as to not piss her off or offend her. "If the police are coming to Burdensville to interview the locals, they are going to ask much more pointed questions than I am, Denise. Don't you think it's vital that you answer them honestly, or do you want people to continue dying?"

Denise stared at him, turning everything over in her mind. "I have to go right now," she said finally. "I'll share my thoughts with you later, probably when I bring your supper."

Scott nodded at her without saying another word. Denise simply turned around and left the jail, locking the door behind her. He knew he had upset her, but if she had the same suspicions as he did, she needed to share them with police. Holding back on the part of anyone in the community would end badly; more people would die, and that was exactly what needed to be avoided.

He grabbed the bag of food and the milk cup and began unpacking it. He was very hungry, and his stomach was growling loudly, but the food was the furthest thing from his mind. His thoughts were focused on Sheriff Darby and the way he responded to him when they first met in the restaurant. He was thinking about how Darby had been willing to go so far as to lock him up over the true offender.

It seemed to Scott that Darby was willing to go to any lengths to protect Ronnie Smith, and that made him think that Ronnie Smith was guilty of much more than drunken, mouthy debauchery.

Scott was willing to bet that either Ronnie Smith or Sheriff Darby himself was the killer, but if it was Ronnie, why would the sheriff be protecting him? It made no sense, no sense at all. Scott's curiosity was piqued, but there was nothing he could do except sit in this jail cell and read newspapers.

But he had a bad feeling about this; a very bad feeling indeed.

∞

Ronnie Smith had taken down the black sheet on the front window first thing that morning. He hadn't had a drink in a couple of days, and for the first time in a long time, he wanted to see and feel the sun.

Bobby had told him he needed to stay inside and out of sight. He told him no driving. He told him he couldn't drink. Ronnie had gotten angry and frustrated at all the orders and demands, but he had agreed. Now, as he sat in the sun thinking about everything, he found himself craving a beer or a shot more than ever.

His head had never been right, and drinking was the only thing that dulled the sting of his torturous mind. His brains just didn't work right, and the thing was that Ronnie wasn't even aware of it. He had the mentality of an eleven or twelve year old, but he was trapped in the body of a thirty-two year old man.

He had always used alcohol to deal with it, and yes, the more he drank the more he lost his inhibitions. That's when the thing inside of him got stronger, and it would demand that he find satisfaction. So that was what he did, it was that simple.

When he was younger, just a boy, the demands in his head had started, and he had dealt with it with the animals that lived in and around town. Yes, he would hurt them, but only for a little bit. Then he would show them mercy by crushing their throats. He would stomp on their necks to end it fast. That was all he would do in the beginning.

But when he got to be a teenager, he had taken things a step further. It wasn't enough just to hurt the local cats and small dogs. Now, he had another hunger inside of him that needed to be satisfied, and it was not a hunger he understood. It was a physical drive, a need for physical release. That was when he started having sex with the animals he killed. That was all Ronnie had done to make the demands in his head stop for many years.

The fact was that all the girls had started to look very, very appealing to him. They smelled good and looked pretty, and those things were enough to drive him crazy. But none of them wanted to talk to him, much less touch him or let him touch them willingly, and it pissed him off. Only a couple short months ago, Ronnie decided he was going to take what he wanted, whether they liked it or not.

The mixture of sex and murder with a human female victim was unlike anything he had ever experienced. They all really loved him, he knew. Just like that last girl, the one he had in the field. So what if she had been with some boy; Ronnie knew she really wanted to be with him, not that kid. He had done her a favor by caving in the boy's skull.

He thought about the way she sounded, the fear in her screams. He thought about her scent, and it started to nag at his brain. He moved his hand to his crotch and began to rub himself through the heavy denim that covered him. While he did this, he thought about how that girl felt on the inside and the terrified look in her eyes, and in only a few moments Ronnie climaxed in his jeans.

As soon as he was done, the feelings came. He felt shame, he felt dirty, and he felt self-hate. It reminded him of mother Smith.

∞

It was the day after his twelfth birthday party, which had been the best one of his life. He had gotten several items of clothing and a new bike, and he was beside himself with eager joy. His mother had told him he could take the bike out and ride it today, but she had gone to do her shopping and forgot to get the new bike out of father's shed. It was locked up, and Ronnie didn't think he could wait.

He suddenly got a brilliant idea. He would go get the key to the shed out of father's desk drawer. He would get his bike out and then lock the shed and return the key. Mother said he could ride it, so she wouldn't be angry. If anything, she would be happy that he did it all by himself.

He went to the den and opened the top drawer in father's desk, where the key was always kept. He pulled the drawer out pretty far, almost pulling it completely from the desk itself. His eyes were on the key, which was nestled in the very front compartment. He steadied the drawer to keep from spilling the contents, and that was when he saw it.

There was a magazine in the back of the drawer, a magazine with shiny paper pages. There on the front was the most beautiful lady he had ever seen. His eyes were immediately glued to it, and the key to the shed was forgotten.

Ronnie took the magazine carefully from the drawer. The woman on the front had hardly any clothes on, and she was so attractive that Ronnie was holding his breath. He began to flip through the pages.

A long page in the middle suddenly folded out, and there was the same girl, but in this picture she was completely naked. Her body looked so soft. He could see everything, even her most secret place. He stared at the photo and let himself plop down into his father's desk chair.

He felt his penis growing harder, and he reached down to adjust it, but as soon as his hand got there the thing sprang up larger than ever. He continued to look at the naked woman as he ran his hand over his crotch, slowly at first, then faster and faster. All of a sudden

Ronnie was overwhelmed with pleasure that ran from the top of his head to the bottom of his feet. He closed his eyes and continued to stroke himself frantically.

"Ronnie, what are you doing?" His eyes flew open to see his mother standing at the door, her mouth and eyes wide. "That's dirty, Ronald! Dirty!"

She ran at him and grabbed him by his hair, dragging him across the room. The magazine had fallen from his hand to the floor, forgotten. All he was aware of was the pain of his hair being pulled.

"Mother, I'm sorry!" He was yelling it over and over. Soon, she had him in the bathroom, and she had turned the shower on full blast. She kept his hair in a firm grip to control him. Ronnie could see the steam rising from the hot water.

"Get in now, Dirty Boy!" The water was too hot, and he knew it. He tried to resist, but mother began to beat him about the head with her other hand, and soon she had forced him into the water. It scalded his skin, and he screamed for mercy.

She got under the sink then and pulled out the brush she used to scrub the floor. She threw it at him hard, the wooden handle knocking him in the head. Then she got the bathtub cleanser out from under there, and she had dumped it all over him.

"Clean yourself! You're filthy and disgusting!" He was so confused and scared that he froze, and mother had grabbed the brush. She scrubbed him all over so hard that his beet-red skin became raw.

He had continued to cry, and she had continued to scrub him and hit him until she drew blood.

∞

Ronnie would never forget what a nasty, dirty boy he was, but the booze helped him put it out of his mind.

Ronnie stood up abruptly, shaking his head violently to rid himself of the memory. He was dirty and disgusting. He needed to wash. He began to tear through the house trying to find the cleanser, but there was none.

That was when he remembered seeing a can of the blue-green powder in the basement. Yes! That's where it was! It was on the very top shelf in the basement, where he had used it in the basement shower to clean himself after he had killed that first girl. He ran through the garbage and debris to the basement door. He flung it open and took the steps down two at a time, his flashlight bobbing erratically.

Now, he shined the light on the top shelf. There it was: the bathroom cleanser that stung and burned. Now, he directed the stream of light around the basement until he saw the metal pail. He grabbed it and turned it upside down before the shelves. He wasn't tall enough to reach without it.

He stepped up and shone the light on the cleanser. He grabbed it up eagerly, relief flooding his body. He would feel better in no time.

There, on the very back of the top shelf, was a bottle of whiskey, and it was three-quarters full.

Ronnie dropped the powdered cleanser to the floor, forgetting it completely. At first, he just stared at the whiskey, but soon his mind started the nagging. Bobby had told him no drinking. That was what Bobby said.

'But Bobby's not here now, is he?' the voice nagged. 'He won't come 'til this weekend, when he comes to do the yard.'

That was all it took. Ronnie grabbed the bottle and took the cap off, then he took a long, hard pull off the bottle. Then another, then another. He stepped down off the pail, a warm feeling coming over him. He didn't remember hiding the bottle, but right then he was so glad he had.

Where had the flashlight gone? He squinted his eyes in the dim light that came through the small windows. It wasn't on the floor. He gently put the bottle down, smiling at it and caressing it slightly, then stepped back on the pail. The flashlight was on the shelf, right where he had left it when he found the whiskey.

The voice was quiet, but he knew it would be back. It always came back. He pushed the thought out of his mind and got down off the pail, grabbed his bottle, and ran up the stairs of the basement.

Ronnie sat down in his place among the filth on the floor. He cracked the bottle once again and took another drink. It warmed him and made him feel loved, and that was all he cared about right then.

He just wanted to feel loved.

CHAPTER 14

Darby sat in the cold, hard chair at the State Police headquarters. His stomach burned with anxiety, and he felt fidgety. It took all of his strength to keep from fiddling around. He didn't want to look as nervous as he felt.

He watched the cops and others who were milling around, taking care of their business. He found he was jealous of all of them. They were oblivious to the weight he was carrying around on his shoulders, and he wished he too was none the wiser. The fact was that he was in trouble, and he knew it.

Gone was his job; maybe not today, but soon enough, that was for sure. He had no idea how to handle the upcoming questions. Should he continue to sidestep and lie to save Ronnie's sick little butt? Even if he did, it wouldn't work. They might not be aware of him now, but all it would take were the interviews of the townsfolk and they would be aware soon enough.

As far as murder goes, suspecting Ronnie was a no-brainer.

He was becoming more and more convinced that it was time to talk. He couldn't continue to do this anymore. Not only was it tearing him apart, it was enabling Ronnie, and people were dying as a result.

Yes, he thought it might be time to show his hand.

As if on cue, the door across from him opened and a man in a suit and tie, with a badge on his belt, nodded at him. "Sheriff Robert Darby?"

Darby stood and nodded curtly. "Yes sir."

"Follow me, please," he said.

The two men walked through the door, and Darby let it shut behind him. His mind was racing and he was a nervous wreck, but he knew what he had to do. His decision to spill the beans gave him great relief. It was the right thing now, and he knew it. If nothing else, maybe they could get Ronnie the help he needed.

It occurred to him right then and there that was exactly what his mother had meant when she told him to take care of his little brother all those years ago. She didn't mean to cover his rear so he had no consequences. She meant that she wanted him to do whatever was best.

The door they had walked through offered a long corridor on the other side, with doors up and down both walls. The two men walked silently down the hall to the last door on the left. Here it is, Darby, he thought to himself. It's time.

They walked inside the room. There was a table at one end, and two men in suits were seated there with laptops open and pens and paper ready to go. A third chair sat empty next to them with the same items on the table before it. A tape recorder sat ready and waiting on the table as well. Before the table was an empty folding chair, obviously meant for him.

"Sheriff, I'm Investigator Frye," said the man who had brought him back. He motioned to the first man at the table. "This is Investigator Garris and Investigator Stein. All three of us will be conducting this interview. Have a seat, please."

Darby sat in the cold metal chair, a serious look on his face. He focused his attention on the men and waited for them to speak. They were all tapping away at their keyboards for a moment, then the man named Garris spoke.

"Are you ready to begin the interview, Sheriff?"

Darby nodded. "I am."

Stein reached out and pressed record on the tape player. "This is the official State Police interview with Sheriff Robert Darby of Burdensville. Present are Investigator Miles Garris, Investigator James Stein, and Investigator Ken Frye of the State Police. Also present is Sheriff Robert Darby."

Darby cleared his throat and waited expectantly.

Frye began. "Sheriff Darby, the line of questions we will be asking are about the recent slew of murders committed in and around Burdensville. Your full cooperation is expected, as we are focused on putting a stop to these killings."

Darby nodded.

"The machine can't record a nod, Sheriff," Frye said sarcastically.

"I understand," Darby replied.

Stein took the ball. "Sheriff Darby, is it true that there have been a total of five murders in the Burdensville area in the last two months?"

"Yes sir, it is," Darby said.

"To date you have not apprehended the killer, nor have you conducted a thorough investigation into any of the deaths?"

He cleared his throat again. "No sir, I have not."

The men exchanged glances before Stein continued. "Can you explain why this is, and why you failed to reach out to any other official agencies for assistance?"

Darby sat quietly for a moment. He looked at each man in the eye, individually. Finally, he took a deep breath and sat back. He was ready.

Darby began to speak.

∞

As expected, Dickie's Café was slammed the next day; as a matter of fact, it was worse than the day before. Denise had taken Scott his lunch around an hour before and returned to work as quickly as possible. The two didn't have time to talk, but she reassured him that she would be back later that night with his supper, and they would visit then.

The customers at every table had wanted the scoop on what was going on in Burdensville, but Denise skillfully sidestepped their questions. Three groups of reporters, all from news networks, came, and their curiosity made it hard for either her or Donna to be productive. It bordered on chaos.

Surprisingly, business began to dwindle down by three in the afternoon. Denise was able to take a quick meal break, and she took the time to think things through. Scott wanted to talk about the murders, and his questions from early that morning had really got her thinking. He was right; she suspected Ronnie Smith. Unless the killer was from out of town, there was no one else she could think of. It would be just like the strange man to do something crazy, and she had heard information over the years that would back up her theory.

Numerous times she had heard gossip that Ronnie went through a bout of killing the townsfolk's pets. She had even heard that he was doing despicable things with their little bodies. She had always chalked it up to just that: gossip.

Then she thought about the day Scott had come to Burdensville and the circumstances that ended him up in jail. She remembered the things Ronnie had said to her, and the look in his drunken eyes when he said them. She had been afraid of him, believing that he was fully capable of hurting her. She had been more frightened of Darby, but now she found that fear had fled.

She wanted to see the killer caught and punished. She wanted to put this situation as far from her mind as she could. If the state police came and did interrogations, she would tell them anything they wanted to know as best as she could. Scott was right, she needed to cooperate.

Denise finished her light lunch of egg salad and a cold milk, then she went back to work. She wanted to get this day behind her, so she could talk to Scott. Then she wanted to go home and lock the doors and spend time with her sister. Soon Diane would be going away, and Denise was beside herself about it.

∞

"Sheriff Darby, are you willing to give a legal statement verifying everything you just told us?" Garris asked. He had just finished telling them everything, and he felt like he had just gotten rid of a hundred pounds of extra weight.

He nodded. "Of course. I do have only one request."

Stein replied, "What would that be?"

"I want to be the one to arrest Ronnie and bring him in," Darby said. "He's done some terrible things, but he is still like a kid. I think, I should be the one."

The investigators all looked at each other, and finally Frye said, "I don't think that will be a problem, considering your cooperation. You're still the sheriff of Burdensville, at least for now."

Darby nodded with relief. Yes, it was only right that he be the one. After all, his negligence had let this thing get out of hand.

CHAPTER 15

Ronnie was seeing double. He looked at the whiskey bottle on the floor before him and saw that there were only about two shots left, and he began to get angry. He was going to have to go to town for more.

The voice in his head began to taunt him then. You're not supposed to drive. You're stuck here, and soon you'll be out of booze. The only way you can get more is to climb in your trusty car and go into town.

No, Ronnie thought. Bobby had told him no. He shook his head violently, trying to clear it, but the voice was just too damn loud.

He grabbed the bottle and held it up to his lips. He guzzled what was left inside easily; then, he threw the glass bottle against the wall, where it shattered to pieces.

He began to laugh hysterically, so hard he actually fell over from a sitting position. Ronnie went with it, then he struggled to sit himself back up. He looked for the bottle; where the hell was it? He finally told himself. He was going to climb into Old Mabel and run to the general mercantile. He wanted to drink more whiskey.

Ronnie stood and made his way out the back door, leaving it hanging open behind him. He staggered a bit, then righted himself and felt in the pocket of his filthy jeans for the key. Once he had it, he started to laugh again; that stupid Bobby should have taken his keys if he didn't want him to drive.

He walked to the back of the dilapidated building where Old Mabel was parked. Next, he started it, put it into gear, and floored the accelerator.

Old Mable crashed through the wall of the building like it was made of paper. Ronnie didn't stop to observe the damage; he didn't give a damn about that building, or about anything but getting a bottle for that matter. He continued to floor it out of his dirt driveway, then he took a sloppy left onto the gravel road leading to town.

He would be at the mercantile shortly, and he thought he might get two bottles instead of one.

∞

Diane Jensen stood on the steps of the Burdensville K-12 talking to her best friend Mandy. "So, why don't you come with us tonight to the bonfire? We're not gonna stay out too late, Di. Tomorrow's a school day."

Diane shook her head, but offered her friend a genuine smile. "Naw, I can't and you know it. I have a paper to work on for chemistry, and I'm supposed to hang out with Denise tonight. She's getting all sentimental that I'm leaving for college in the fall, so I have to go home."

Mandy shrugged. "Well, girl, if anything changes give me a call. We can jump in Connor's truck and come get you."

"Fine," she replied. "I'll see you tomorrow, okay?"

The two girls parted ways, and Diane began to walk home. The school was on the very edge of town, and the walk took her about fifteen minutes if she went straight home. Today, she had to stop at the mercantile and pick up a pack of black pens. Her last one had given up on her during last period.

She walked in a leisurely manner until she reached the store. Parked outside was that old beater car that belonged to that weirdo Ronnie Smith. He always made her nervous the way he looked at her. It was like the things he was thinking about her were about to make him drool. He was not only weird, he was smelly and disgusting, too.

She pulled on the heavy door and the bell rang. Mildred Castner, the store's owner, was at the single register.

"Hey, Diane, what can I get for you today?" Mildred was a large woman with a beautiful face and a spirit to match. Just hearing her voice made Diane smile.

"Just some pens today. I'll grab them." She walked down the aisle where the school and office supplies were located. Her pens were right there, and she grabbed two packs instead of one.

"Hey, you," she heard the voice from behind. "Pretty girl…. you're a pretty one."

Diane spun around, the hair on the back of her neck standing up. Ronnie Smith stood there smiling. She smelled him even before she saw him; his clothes were covered in filth, and he looked like he hadn't bathed in months. The smell of booze came off him in waves.

"Hi, Ronnie," she said timidly. "Good to see you. I gotta be getting on now." She turned around and headed to Mildred and the register.

But Ronnie barged past her, then laughed at himself. "Ima wanna go first," he told her. "Ima in a hurry."

Diane let out a sigh of relief. Good, go ahead, she thought. The last thing she wanted was for this guy gawking at her or following her home. She watched as he lurched toward Mildred and steadied himself on the counter. The woman jerked backward as she got a nose full of him.

"Gimme two bottles of that there mash," Ronnie breathed. He was digging through his pockets for money.

Mildred got a concerned look on her face. "You seem pretty good already, Ronnie, ayuh."

The man withdrew a wad of bills from his pocket and slammed them on the counter. Either he hadn't heard her or he didn't care what she had to say. "Two of 'em now," he repeated.

Mildred looked torn. She was like everyone else in town; they all knew Ronnie could make trouble for them. She exchanged looks with Diane then turned around and grabbed two pints of whiskey from the shelf behind the counter. She punched the numbers into the register. "Sixteen eighty-five, Ronnie."

The man shoved the bills across the countertop and held his hands out eagerly. "Don't you want a bag, Ron?"

"Nah. Don't need no bag," he said. He took the bottles and turned around to face Diane. "You wanna come with me an' have a l'il sippy?"

Diane scrunched her nose up with distaste, and Ronnie noticed. "No thanks, Ronnie," she answered, forcing a smile. "I have a paper due tomorrow in school, and I have to get it done."

Ronnie's eyes clouded over and he whirled around. With that he was gone, leaving the bell tinkling behind him.

Diane approached the counter and gave Mildred a smile as she laid her packages of pens down. "That guy always gives me the creeps."

"I know, right?" Mildred replied. "Most say he's harmless, but I remember otherwise. Did you know that when he was a kid he was going around killing people's pets? It's also said he would do, you know, sexual things with them."

Diane gave Mildred a look of disgust. "I've heard rumors, too, so I just try to dodge him if I can."

"That's your best bet," the store owner replied. "That'll be three dollars and forty-two cents, sweetie. How's your sister lately?"

Diane paid the woman and picked up the pens. "She's good. She's been super busy down at the café, what with the murders and all."

"Yeah, nothing draws the lowlifes quite like horrible crime." Mildred shut the door to the till and handed the girl a dollar fifty-eight in change for a five. "Well, good luck on your paper, doll. We'll see you later."

Diane walked out into the sun and started for home. She saw a couple of classmates on the other side of the street and gave them a wave then continued on. She loved her afternoon walks home, especially in spring. The wind would blow through her long hair and the sun kissed her skin. Her life was good.

∞

She made it home in no time, and rooted around for the key to the front door. It took her a minute to find it; it had gone to the bottom of her bag. Once she got it in her hand, she slid the key in the lock and opened the door.

The house was still. Perfect, really, for the work she had to do on her paper. She tossed her bag onto the couch and shut the door behind her. She would grab a quick snack and get down to business.

Suddenly, she smelled him, and she knew he was behind her before he ever grabbed her. Her reflexes were poor, though, even dealing with Ronnie in the state he was in. His arm came around and he put her in a tight headlock, then ran his nasty tongue up the side of her face. "You shoulda just had one l'il sippy with me. Jus' one."

Diane began to fight in earnest, but his arm just tightened around her neck and he fought her back. He was so strong, and he was flinging her around as if she were a five pound bag of potatoes. A lamp crashed to the floor off an end table near the door, along with a couple of other knick-knacks. Both of them fell over the couch, and his grip tightened even more.

"Don't fight, Pretty," he breathed. "Just be still; be still."

She couldn't breathe, and she was getting dizzy from the lack of oxygen. Ronnie could tell she was getting weaker, and he tightened his arm around her even more. She was beginning to see stars, and she could feel his other hand fumbling with the button on her jeans.

Diane Jensen jerked in his arms and then lost consciousness. Ronnie continued to squeeze as he violated her with his fingers, and he didn't let up until he was sure the girl was dead. He laid her body clumsily on the floor and brushed her hair out of her face. "Pretty one you are," he mumbled as he tore her clothes from her body.

Ronnie had his way with the girl's body for the next hour, and by the time he was finished, he had sobered up quite a bit. He pulled his filthy jeans up and looked around the room. The reality of what he had just done hit him like a ton of bricks: he had just killed one of the townsfolk.

He looked around the house in a panic, and then went out the same way he came in: through a back window. He had parked his car a couple of blocks away, and the girls had a privacy fence around their back yard. He would be able to get away easily, but there was no way he could ever go home.

∞

Sheriff Darby signed his statement to the state police with flair. He felt nothing but relief about what he had done. It didn't even matter if he lost his job; he would relocate and start over. Good riddance to bad rubbish.

Garris took the statement from him and then sat back in his chair. The other two officers were in the same relaxed position. They were all looking at him, but it was Garris who was showing the most concern.

"Are you going to be all right?" he asked Darby.

Darby took a deep breath and let it out, nodding at the man as he did so. "Yep. I'll be fine. It's all for the best this way, for everyone."

The three cops nodded in agreement, but didn't directly respond to him. Finally, Stein broke the silence. "So, you head back to Burdensville and pick him up, Darby. Bring him directly to the main County jail. We'll contact them and let them know to expect you before the night is over." He looked Darby over carefully once more. "If they don't have the prisoner by midnight, we're gonna have to issue a warrant for your arrest as well, Darby."

"I understand," he said in a low voice. He put his hat on his head and stood to his feet. "It has to be done, and I need to be the one to do it."

The three investigators stood and shook his hand. "Are you sure you don't want an escort from another officer?" Frye asked.

"Nah," Darby replied. "If it's just me it will go a lot more smoothly. If anyone else comes, well, I'm afraid of how he might react."

The men nodded and all of them left the room. Frye escorted Darby out to his patrol car. "We'll be waiting to hear from the jail. You're making the right decision, Darby." He patted him on the shoulder. "You're doing the right thing."

"I know it; I know." With that he unlocked the cruiser and heaved his large frame behind the wheel. "You'll get word soon," he concluded, and then drove away.

R.W.K. Clark

CHAPTER 16

The café was dead after a day being packed once again. Denise, Donna, and Dickie weren't in as high of spirits as they had been the evening before, but they were all relieved that the day was finally over. The girls sat in their regular booths, separating tips and balancing the register while Dickie prepared Scott Sharp's supper for Denise to take to him.

"Wonder what happened with Sheriff Darby today," Donna said. "I'm pretty sure we're gonna be getting a new cop in town."

Denise folded her stack of bills together and put them in her coin purse. "Yeah, I have the same feeling. But if Darby was negligent, then it is something that needs to be done."

"I know," Donna replied. "But it sure is gonna be strange not having Bobby Darby as our sheriff."

Dickie put Styrofoam boxes in the window, and Denise stood up. "Guess it's time for me to get this over there to him. He's probably pretty hungry. I also promised Diane that we would hang out tonight, and Scott wants to chat, so I gotta get moving."

She packed up his food and drink, put her jacket on, and shouted through the window, "I'm out of here, Dickie. See you in the morning?"

"I wouldn't have it any other way," the man replied. "Don't you stay down at the hoosegow too long, now. There's still a crazy man running around out there somewhere, and I can't afford to lose you."

Denise gave a hearty laugh. "Always thinking about the bottom line, aren't you."

"Yeah, well somebody has to."

She left the café and headed directly to the jail. The night was very still, almost creepy, and there was something unsettling about it. The streetlights made the corners look surreal, and Denise was uncomfortable, but she couldn't put her finger on why.

She got to the jail quickly and let herself in. Scott was sitting on his bunk when she came, and he smiled at her when he saw her. "Look, Denise," he began. "I'm sorry for giving you pressure earlier this morning. I don't have any business pushing anyone."

Denise brought the food to him and then sat down in the folding chair. She took off her work shoes and began to rub her feet. "No worries, Scott," she replied. "You were right."

He had sat down on the bed and was unpacking his food. When she said that he looked up, startled. "I was?"

She nodded. "You were. All you did was say what everyone in town is already thinking. I believe all of us have fallen into the habit of looking the other way when it came to the sheriff and Ronnie."

Denise grew thoughtful for a moment, then continued. "There has always been something… unhealthy about their relationship. In a town this size you learn to go with it, whatever it is. I appreciate that you made me think."

Scott tore into his food and they sat in silence for a while. It was a comfortable silence, though. Denise watched him as he ate, and a smile played on her lips as she did. "You sure are a cutie, you know that?" she blushed at her own words, but she was too damn tired to care about what he thought at that point.

He finished quickly and approached the bars. "Thanks for not holding a grudge," he said. "You mentioned spending some time with your sister tonight. I'm not gonna keep you, but I do want to thank you for all you've been doing for me."

Denise put her shoes back on. "No problem. You have actually made my life more interesting." She stood then and came close to him. "I have to say, I'm going to miss you when you're gone."

She leaned forward and put her lips firmly to his. His mouth tasted sweet, so she began to explore his lips with her tongue. She wished she could put her arms around him and pull him to her, and he was thinking the same thing.

The kiss lasted, and it was wonderful. By the time she pulled away, she was breathless. She reached through the bars and tousled his hair. "I'll see you in the morning, Scott Sharp, unless the sheriff says otherwise. By the way, I will be talking to the cops if they come to town to interview."

He watched her walk to the door, clinging to the bars as if he could go right through them and get closer to her. She opened the door and turned around and winked at him. "Sure would be nice if we could spend some real time together."

"It's not like I'm kicked out of town," Scott replied. "At least, not yet." He winked back at her. "Oh, and hey. Will you shut the lights out tonight?"

Denise smiled and did as he wished, then she left and shut the door behind her, locking it. Her mind went to Diane; she planned for them to make homemade pizza together, and maybe watch a movie or play Scrabble.

With that she began the walk home, humming and smiling to herself as she went.

∞

Sheriff Darby's cruiser sliced through the darkness as he made his way back to Burdensville. He thought about his day with the state investigators, and he considered the statement he had given them. He had been so dishonest for so long that he had forgotten what it felt like to do the right thing. He had forgotten the reason he became a cop in the first place.

Once he had resigned himself to getting honest, the only thing he was worried about was Dr. Ivan Smith.

He had helped Darby to brush the murders under the legal rug, and Darby felt a certain amount of guilt for snitching him off. But he knew the facts, and the facts were that they had both done wrong, and now the chips had to fall where they may. Both he and Smith had done deeds that had resulted in ongoing death and destruction, and they both deserved what they got.

He felt lighter and freer than he had in years. He even began to hum an old song as he drove through the dark, and it wasn't until he neared the turn that led to Ronnie's that he began to sober up a bit. His nerves began to tense up, and he knew it was time to get the appropriate attitude. He couldn't let a promise he made to his dead mother thirty-two years ago affect his decision to do the right thing.

Darby took the appropriate left onto the gravel road and put on his brights. His heart was beating faster, and his hands were even shaking a bit, but his confidence in his decision was steadfast. He wanted the murdering Ronnie to pay a consequence. It had to be done.

He finally reached Ronnie's and pulled a left into the dirt drive. His bright lights flashed across the outbuilding to the right rear of the house, and for a second, his mind was unable to register what he was seeing. As a matter of fact, he was sure he was hallucinating.

"What the heck?" He stopped the cruiser and put it in reverse, then put it in drive and put the headlights on the outbuilding. Oh, dang, he thought, his mouth hanging open.

The entire wall of the out building was gone. In its place was a gaping hole, and splintered wood was everywhere. He stared in disbelief, trying to reason out what could have caused the sight. That was when he realized that Old Mabel was not inside the building, as she should have been.

Darby slammed the cruiser into park and grabbed his Mag-Lite. He jumped almost effortlessly from the driver's door, the beam from the flashlight on the back of the outbuilding. He approached it with haste, his heart pounding as he neared.

"Oh, no," he said. "No, please no." By the time he reached the building, there was no denying it: the car was gone, and Ronnie had driven it right through the side of the building.

Now, Darby was nearly panicking. If Ronnie had gone to this extreme, he was drunk. Sober Ronnie would have never done something like this; Old Mabel was his pride and joy, even though it was a piece of junk. The sheriff turned toward the house. The lights were all off, and a quick shine of the flashlight told him that the back door was wide open.

"Ronnie!" Darby was jogging toward the house. "Ronnie, it's Bobby. Where are you, boy?"

He was met with nothing but silence, and the silence was so loud it made him want to scream. He went through the back door and shined his light around the filthy kitchen. He could smell Ronnie in this place, and it made him want to gag.

"Ronnie?" Darby moved through the kitchen and into the living room, where he carefully exposed everything to the light. Right by the front window was a shattered whiskey bottle, and Darby was sure it had not been there the last time he was here. "Oh, no. Damn it."

Darby knew with sick surety that another body would be found in the next day or two.

This was all his fault, and he knew it. Ronnie should have been put out of his misery as soon as they realized what a sick bastard he really was. But Darby knew they were twenty years too late.

Finally he pulled himself up. He had to get it together. Ronnie was out there somewhere. He would go to the jail and use the jail phone to call the state police. He would have to also get ahold of Judge Rupert Allen and request a warrant.

Darby left the house quickly, almost at a run, and got into the cruiser. He put his top lights on, whipped a donut, and then aimed the cruiser out of the drive, taking a left on the gravel toward town. He had to get moving, and he had to figure out where Ronnie might be right now.

∞

Ronnie Smith wasn't as dumb as everyone believed; at least, he didn't think so. He got out of the Jensen house in broad daylight without being seen. He took Old Mabel out to the deserted farmhouse where he had killed that first girl, and he parked in the dilapidated barn. Now he was inside the house, which was nothing more than a skeleton. He had his trusty flashlight, and he had two pints of whiskey; they wouldn't ever find him here.

But he got cold, and the chill made him decide to build a fire. He figured if he built it at the rear of the house, away from the highway, that it wouldn't be seen. He gathered some sticks from outside and got a small fire going, then he sat down by it to warm up. He cracked his first pint and took a nice, long drink. The amber liquid warmed him almost immediately, and after another long pull, he started to not care whether they found him or not.

He hadn't done anything wrong, after all. That damn Jensen girl had looked at him like he was garbage, and all he had done was ask her if she wanted a drink of his hootch. He took another pull from his bottle and leaned his back against the outside wall. He was feeling toasty now, so he closed his eyes and tried to recall every second he had spent in the Jensen house with Diane. She had been the best one yet, and he didn't care who knew it.

Ronnie smiled to himself and began to sing his favorite song.

CHAPTER 17

Denise had left the jail feeling really good about everything. She knew she could be honest with police without fear; Scott had helped to build her confidence, whether he knew it or not. She also felt incredible about Scott himself. Now would be the perfect time to get to know a man. After all, Diane would be leaving in the fall, and she would be able to do things she had refused to do while her little sister was in her care.

She was so proud of the young lady Diane had become. She smiled as she considered the girl and her future, and her smile was still on her face when she turned the key in the lock on the front door of their little house. She was excited to spend an hour or two with the girl, even if it was a little late to watch a movie. It was a school night, after all.

She turned the knob to the door at the exact moment that it registered in her mind that none of the lights in the house were on. Had Diane gone on to bed? Maybe she was overwhelmed about her chemistry assignment. Oh, well, Denise thought, there was always tomorrow, and tomorrow was Friday.

She reached to her left to turn the lamp on that sat on the end table, but she groped fruitlessly in the dark. "Diane? I'm home!" she shouted.

The smell hit her first. It was a smell she knew all too well. It was a mix of sweat and booze and bodily filth. It was the smell of Ronnie Smith.

Now, she began to feel along the wall for the overhead light switch. It came on and hurt her eyes, which she fluttered rapidly as they adjusted.

Then Denise saw her. At first, she thought her sister had decided to sleep on the living room floor, just to bother her. She hated that, and Diane knew it.

But something wasn't right. She was naked, and she had no pillow or blanket. Her eyes were wide open, and she stared lifelessly into nothingness.

"Diane?" she ran to the body then, and immediately began screaming at the top of her lungs. "Diane! Wake up!" She grabbed the girl's bare shoulders and began to shake her hard, but Diane didn't feel anything anymore.

Denise was in shock. Her first thought was to call the sheriff, so she ran to the phone and dialed the number. It rang and rang. She slammed the phone down in frustration and ran out the front door.

"Help! Somebody help me!" She continued to scream as she began to run in the direction of the jail. She could use the radio system there to get ahold of state police. She could dig through the sheriff's desk to find the spare key to the cell, and she could let Scott out, so he could help her wake Diane.

Denise was making no sense in her mind. She was borderline hysterical, and she continued to scream as she ran. A couple of lights came on in a couple of different homes, but she didn't even notice. Within minutes she was at the jail, and she was taking the keys from her apron to unlock the door.

Right then Sheriff Robert Darby pulled up in his cruiser, lights flashing.

"Denise!" he yelled. He immediately noticed her distress; she couldn't find the right key, and she was crying and sobbing hysterically. Darby grabbed her. "What's going on? What's wrong, Denise."

She looked at him, eyes wide. "Diane! He's killed Diane! Now, we have to call an ambulance!"

"Who did, Denise? Who killed Diane?"

Denise whirled on him, her eyes mad. "My house stinks like Ronnie Smith!"

With that she fainted dead away.

Darby caught her in his arms just in the nick of time. As he stood holding her up, jail keys in one hand, the gravity of her words hit him. Was she saying Ronnie was in her home? Was she saying Diane was dead, and that Ronnie was the reason?

He continued to hold her up with one arm and with the other hand he unlocked the jail door. Darby reached around the door frame and flipped on the overhead lights inside to see Scott standing up against the bars.

"What the heck is going on?" He had heard the commotion outside but couldn't make out the words.

The sheriff proceeded to haul Denise's small body into the building, where he then sat her in one of the chairs near the door. He turned to Scott as he caught his breath.

"I've done a terrible thing, and I need your help."

Now Scott was nearly out of his mind with concern. "What's going on Sheriff Darby?"

The sheriff headed directly for his cell. He opened the door and let Scott out. "It's a long story, but the gist of it is that you shouldn't even be here. I have to call the state police for assistance, then I need your help, Mr. Sharp."

Darby grabbed the phone from its cradle and proceeded to punch in a series of numbers. Scott ran over to where Denise was seated in a chair slumped over. When he realized that she was out cold, he looked around the room desperately. He remembered a small refrigerator was situated behind the sheriff's desk, and he ran to it. Inside were some cans of soda, a couple containers of vanilla yogurt, and a single bottle of water that was half empty. Scott grabbed the bottle and ran back to take care of Denise.

"This is Sheriff Robert Darby of Burdensville. I need to speak with the duty officer immediately please. It is an emergency." Darby turned to see Scott pour water into his own cupped palms and splash it onto Denise's ashen face.

"Hello, Officer Keating. This is Sheriff Robert Darby of Burdensville. I have a report of a murder, and the suspect is one that I was to bring in to you to

Somerset County by midnight. We don't know where he is, and we have a dead girl here in town."

Scott looked over his shoulder anxiously. A dead girl? Denise passed out from shock?

Darby continued. "Yes. I need backup. I'm going to be beginning a search of the immediate area around town. I know the subject well, and I have some ideas where he might be hiding." He paused for a moment, then continued. "Yes, I'll radio if I find anything. Thanks. See your men soon."

He hung up the phone and turned to Scott. "Denise said Diane Jensen is dead. I need you to come with me to find Ronnie Smith. I have no other officers."

Denise's eyes began to flutter open and for a brief moment, she looked confused. "Where… what?"

Scott spoke to her soothingly. "Denise, I need you to lie down in my cell, and I need you to stay there."

The look on her face changed drastically as her memory came back to her. She jumped up, but was unsteady on her feet, and Scott had to help her sit back down. "We have to get to Diane. She won't wake up."

"Denise, we are going to go there now," he replied. "I need you to stay here and hold down the fort because the state police are on their way."

Darby dialed another number and paced as he waited for his party to pick up. "Ivan, it's Bobby," he said into the receiver. "I need you right away at the Jensen residence." He paused again. "I'll fill you in when you get there."

Scott had Denise in the cell, and she was sitting on the edge of his cot. "I want to come with you!" Tears were falling freely from her eyes now as she recalled the situation.

"Listen Denise," he told her gently, "I need you to stay here. We're going to your house to take care of Diane now, but you have to stay here, okay?"

She nodded, a confused look on her face, then she threw herself into Scott's pillow and began to sob in earnest. Scott turned to Darby. "Let's go."

The two men left the jail, with Darby making sure the building was secure behind them. They jumped into the cruiser and sped off, heading for Denise's home. "We need to see exactly what she is talking about," Darby said. "But I'm pretty sure of what we are going to find."

Scott was furious with the sheriff. "I guess, I just don't understand how a man of the law could sweep this type of crap under the rug for so long. What the heck is wrong with you, anyway?"

Darby shot a glare in his direction, but Scott could see the guilt and shame in his eyes as well. "I don't expect you to understand, but there is a lot more to it than you realize. All I can do is deal with the here and now, and believe me, there are consequences I am going to have to suffer for my bad decisions, so mind your own business."

"Well, you've pretty much made it my business at this point," Scott retorted.

They pulled up in front of Denise's small white bungalow. A man with a bag and a jacket was standing on the sidewalk. "Dr. Smith," Darby muttered as the two of them climbed quickly from the cruiser and approached the doctor.

"Thanks for getting here so fast, Ivan," Darby began. "I got back to town with the intent of arresting Ronnie. I'm supposed to deliver him over to the State, but instead of Ronnie, I found Denise Jensen. She's hysterical; she says Diane is dead inside the house."

"Well, let's see what we have," Ivan Smith replied.

The three of them went up to the house, and Darby opened the screen door. The overhead light in the living room was still on, and the door was wide open. "Police!" he shouted, hand on his gun. "We're coming inside!" He knew it was a long shot that Ronnie would be there; if he were still around, Darby didn't have a doubt that Denise wouldn't have stood a chance either.

The men entered the house to see Diane in the same position that Denise had discovered her. "Shit," Darby said, his eyes closed in disgust. Ivan Smith jumped into action and grabbed an afghan from the back of the sofa. He knelt next to the girl and closed her eyes, then covered her body.

Darby turned to Scott, whose eyes were flaring with rage and dismay. "I can't believe I let this go so far."

"She was just a baby. I can't believe it either." Scott shook his head. "We need to find Ronnie, and we need to do it now before anyone else has to pay this steep of a price."

Darby nodded and wiped his face with his shirtsleeve. "Ivan, Scott and I are going to go check a couple of places outside of town. I've already been to Ronnie's place; his car is gone, and I found a broken booze bottle that wasn't there before, so I know he's trashed. There are a few places I believe he could be. You stay here and wait for the state police, if you would."

The doctor gave him a nod, his face grief stricken. He knew that his role in covering Ronnie's murders had led to this, just as Darby's had. He was disgusted with the entire situation, and he was ready to throw in the towel. "Of course, Bobby, of course."

Darby and Scott got into the cruiser and left. "So," Scott began, "what makes you think you're gonna be able to track him down? Heck, he could be in Timbuktu by now."

"Yep," Darby replied, "But what you don't understand is that I know Ronnie better than anyone. He's never been out of Burdensville in his life. We'll go by his house one more time, but I don't expect to find him there. There are few places he could truly hide near home. There is a vein of the Allagash River just outside of town here; Ronnie fished there pretty regularly up until he was a teen, then he just stopped. I figure he'll either be there or at the old Wilson farm."

"Why would he go someplace to hide that you would be able to figure out?" Scott asked.

She sheriff turned to him, a resigned look on his face. "He has the mentality of a twelve year old, Sharp. He's not going to be able to reason effectively at all. Besides, there is no other place for him to go."

"Why did you let yourself get involved with this in the first place, Darby?" Scott questioned. "Why not leave it to his brother Ivan?"

Darby took a deep ragged breath. "Doc Smith isn't his brother, Sharp," Darby replied. "I am."

"What? What the heck are you talking about?"

So Darby told Scott the brief version, if there was one, of the truth behind who Ronnie was to Darby and how he managed to become so twisted and distorted in the way he protected the man. He wrapped it up as they pulled into the dirt drive at Ronnie's house.

"Everything just snowballed, and I let it happen, but I'm gonna make it right now," he concluded.

Darby parked the cruiser but left it running. "You stay here; I'm just gonna give the house a quick run through once more. I don't expect he's here, so I'll only be a minute." He grabbed his flashlight and headed for the house.

Scott was in shock himself, and he was struggling to comprehend the mess that had been made in Burdensville by the sheriff and the doctor. Sure, he had listened closely to Darby's story, but he felt no compassion for the law man. He had allowed and covered up all those murders, and the result had been more death and grief. He only hoped the sheriff meant it when he said he was ready to make it right.

Poor Denise! He hadn't known her long, but what he had learned about her was that her sister Diane had been her whole life. He closed his eyes and shook his head. How did his travels bring him to a town and a situation like this?

Darby was back quickly. He jumped into the cruiser and put it in gear. "No dice; he ain't here." He backed out of the drive, and soon they were headed up the gravel road to Highway 16. "I'm going to take us to the Allagash; we'll be passing the Wilson place on the way, so we'll stop and check that too. The State Police should be arriving soon; they'll be getting in touch with me on the radio any time, and that's when the real searching will start."

Darby was anxious to find Ronnie before anyone else got killed.

CHAPTER 18

Scott took a breath. "Look, Darby," he began, "I'm not comfortable helping you look for this madman without some kind of protection. I mean heck, you have a gun, and all I have are my fists. I've never killed anyone, but your brother has, and I'm pretty sure he won't hesitate to try to kill me."

Darby winced visibly at Scott's loose 'madman' reference, but what could he say? The guy was right; Ronnie was out of his mind. "I'll let you use the rifle." He jerked his head backward toward the gun that hung on the safety glass that separated the back seat from the front.

"Thanks sheriff," Scott replied. He was keeping his eyes to the windows, staring out into the darkness that hid everything they needed to see. He didn't want to miss any sign of life out here, because any sign was likely going to be Ronnie this far out in the sticks at this time of night.

"Up here about half a mile on the right is the Wilson farm. The Allagash is another five miles past that, and we're gonna have to hike a bit to get to his old fishing spot," Darby said. "Just keep your eyes peeled."

Scott nodded vaguely. "I already am."

A house came into view on the right, but just barely. All Scott could see was its shadowy skeleton. He strained his eyes at it as it drew nearer, and that was when he saw light flickering off an outbuilding at the rear of the place. "Slow down, Sheriff, I see a light."

"At the house?" The sheriff slowed the cruiser. "I don't see nothin'."

Scott began to point into the night. "Not bright light. Look," he thrust his pointer finger toward the house as he tried to show Darby. "It's flickering off that barn or garage or whatever it is. In the back, there!"

Darby saw it then; it was so subtle that if he hadn't had Scott with him, he would likely have never noticed it. "Ayuh," he replied as he pulled the cruiser to the shoulder of the road. "Someone's there alright. I don't know if you know it or not, but this is where Ronnie's first victim was found. I'm not surprised; it's gonna be him."

Darby left the cruiser running and turned to Scott. "This is gonna be hard for me. I just want you to know. He is my brother, and I love him, so it's gonna be hard."

"I understand," Scott replied, "But you need to get over it."

Darby nodded and took a deep breath. He turned around and took the gun from its rack on the safety glass. "You know how to shoot?"

"A little," Scott replied.

Finally, they were ready to head up to the abandoned house and the light that flickered there.

"Now, don't slam the car doors when we get out, got it?" Darby was already whispering, and they were still in the car.

"Got it," Scott said. "Listen, if it looks to me like you're losing your nerve, I'm gonna act, Sheriff. I can't get the picture of that dead girl out of my mind; this guy needs to be caught."

"Fine. Let's go," said Darby.

The two men got out of the cruiser and shut the car doors slowly and carefully. They got their guns ready to be used and headed quietly up the slight hill to the empty house atop of it. That was when Scott heard the singing.

"Darby, stop!" He whispered as he reached out and touched Darby's arm. "Do you hear that?"

"Hear what?"

Scott was straining to hear. "Listen!"

They took a few more steps forward, then Darby heard it. Ronnie was singing, and it was obvious he was drunk. He slurred his words terribly as he sang them, and he couldn't keep his tune...

Darby and Scott looked at each other in the darkness. "He's around the house, in the back," Darby whispered. "You go around that way, and I'll go opposite. Now listen, I wanna try to take him alive, I wanna try to reason and talk to him, so when you get back there, try to not let him see you right away. He's liable to get upset after what happened between you two at the café, alright?"

"I'll stay out of it unless I have to get in it," Scott replied, then he took off to the right of the house and Darby went left.

The two men came around the rear at the same time. Scott stopped, poised frozen with the rifle. There sat Ronnie, at a small fire he had built. In the light of the fire, Scott could see that he had a pint of booze in his left hand, and he was swinging it back and forth to the screwed up rhythm of the song he sang. Next to him, on the ground, was another pint bottle. It was empty, and the bottom had been broken off.

He was good and drunk, Ronnie was.

Darby had his gun pointed at the man, and from where Scott was standing, he could see that the man's hand was shaking. "Ronnie," Darby said gently, "what are you doin' out here all alone?"

Ronnie stopped singing right away, and he jerked his head to his left to look at Sheriff Darby.

"What you doin' here, Bobby?" His voice was almost like that of a child.

Darby cleared his throat. "I come to take you home, Ronnie."

"What-cha got that gun for then?"

The sheriff took a small step toward the man who was his biological brother. "Ronnie, what did you do?"

Ronnie put the pint to his lips and took a draw off it. "I ain't doin' nothin'. Just having a fire, Bobby." He tried to get to his feet, but he seemed to be having a hard time standing. He fell back on his butt hard, then pushed himself up again. It was slow going, but he finally made it to his feet. Scott kept the rifle pointed at the killer, but kept his mouth shut.

"Now Ronnie," Darby continued, "I know what you did today."

Ronnie gave a hearty drunken laugh. "Ha! You don' know nuthin'."

"Yes, Ronnie. Yes I do," said Darby, his voice taking on a slightly stern tone. "You saw Diane Jensen today, didn't you, Ronnie?"

Ronnie's face scrunched up as if he were struggling to find the mental file on Diane Jensen. Suddenly his eyes lit up. "Pretty, pretty girl."

"What did you do, Ronnie?" The sheriff's voice was sinister and quiet.

Ronnie put the pint to his lips and drained the last of the whiskey from the glass bottle before lobbing it as hard as he could into the darkness. It hit the ground with a small 'thud' a short distance away. Then he turned his attention back on Darby. "I wanted to share with her, but she wouldn't share with me. I visited her house, I did."

"What did I tell you about drinking, Ronnie?" The sheriff was taking small steps toward the man, and so far Ronnie hadn't noticed. "See what happens when you drink? You killed that girl, Ronnie."

Now the man shook his head violently, his eyes closed. "No! She wanted me to visit; she wanted to be with me." By the time he opened his eyes again, Darby was only a few feet away from him.

"You have to come with me now, Ronnie," Darby said firmly.

He shook his head again. "I'm stayin' here now; I'm stayin' here."

Darby began to reach out toward the man to take him by the arm, but it seemed that the wasted Ronnie already expected it. In a flash he swung his arm, and the next thing any of them knew he had knocked Darby's gun out of his hand and out of sight. Suddenly the two men were on the ground struggling.

Scott jumped into action. He ran over to the fighting men, who were right next to the small fire Ronnie had made. The man was on top of the sheriff, his arms flailing as he hit Darby in the head over and over again. Scott tried to aim his gun at Ronnie only, but the men were fighting so hard that he knew if he shot Ronnie, he was going to shoot Darby as well.

Scott was beginning to panic; he didn't have a lot of experience with guns, and he vowed silently to himself that if he ever got out of this, he was going to learn. As he was thinking those thoughts, Ronnie reached out like a flash, and the next thing Scott saw was the jagged broken pint bottle in his hand. Ronnie had ahold of it by its short neck. He swung the glass at Darby's head, and Darby dodged him. He swung it again, and again.

The third swing found its target. The broken glass tore into Darby's neck and ripped it apart. Blood shot from him into the air, and in the firelight Scott could see the stream splatter across Ronnie's face. He continued to swing, but Darby wasn't fighting anymore. His hands had gone up to his neck, his eyes wide with shock as blood pumped through his fingers.

"No!" Scott screamed, and for the first time Ronnie realized that he and his brother were not alone. He fell backwards off the bleeding man in a panic, his arms and legs trying desperately to back him away from Scott and the rifle.

Scott had the rifle trained on the man's head. Ronnie stared at him, open-mouthed. "It's you. You're that man from the café, aintcha?" His voice was trembling with fear, and suddenly he appeared very sober.

The rifle shook in Scott's hands. "Yeah, I'm the one, and now you're coming with me, Ronnie. You should have listened to the sheriff. You should have listened."

The sheriff gave a gurgle, and Scott shifted his gaze in the man's direction, just in time to see him breathe his last. He looked back at Ronnie, sick and furious.

"Now look what you've done, you crazy sicko!" Scott screamed. "You just killed the only person that gave a crap about you!"

Ronnie stood, his movements clumsy and his legs shaky. He looked down at Darby then back at Scott. "I ain't goin' no place."

Scott thought about the pretty blonde girl lying dead at Denise's house. He thought about all the murders he had read about in the paper. Rage built up inside of him as it all ran through his mind.

"You're right, Ronnie," he said. "You're not going anywhere."

Scott pulled the trigger of the rifle, and the projectile tore through Ronnie's head, making it appear to explode before Scott's eyes. Ronnie seemed to be staring at Scott with confusion as he staggered to the right. Suddenly, his body crumpled under his own feet, and he fell on his face into the fire.

Scott dropped the rifle to the ground and knelt down by Darby's body. "Darby?" he said once, but even as he said it, he knew the man was gone.

He fetched Darby's flashlight from the ground where it had fallen when Ronnie first swung and knocked the gun from Darby's hand. He made his way around the house and down the hill to where the cruiser was parked. He could hear the car radio going crazy inside, so he opened the passenger door and sat in the front seat.

"Sheriff Darby, are you still local?" The voice coming from the radio was that of a female.

Scott picked up the mike and pressed the button on the side. "This is Scott Sharp. The sheriff has been killed. So has Ronnie Smith."

The woman's voice replied. "Tell me where you are and we'll get the units there right away."

"I'm at an abandoned farmhouse out on Highway 16, about five miles from Burdensville." He released the button and leaned his head back against the head rest. His heart was trying to return to its normal speed, but it was still going way too fast, and he was panting.

"Officers are in Burdensville; I'll give them your twenty," the woman replied. "Stay right where you are."

He pressed the button and said, "I ain't goin' no place." When he realized he had just repeated Ronnie's last words, Scott laughed as though he had just told the funniest joke of his life.

CHAPTER 19

Burdensville Sheriff Killed During Attempted Apprehension. Recent Murders Solved.

Sheriff Robert Darby of Burdensville was killed while trying to apprehend the man suspected of being responsible for six murders that recently took place in and around the town. Ronald W. Smith of Burdensville is said to have raped and killed a handful of people in recent months, including travelers and one local high school girl.

State Police had been conducting an investigation into Darby, who was accused of negligence and using poor investigative tactics. According to police spokeswoman Mary Kay Monroe, the sheriff had just given police a thorough statement about Smith and the murders. Darby was ordered to locate the suspect and take him immediately to the County for detention. Both the sheriff and the suspect were killed when the arrest was attempted.

Scott Sharp of Coos Bay, Oregon was with Darby during the incident. According to Sharp, Smith killed Diane Jensen, 17, of Burdensville, then hid at an abandoned farm on the outskirts of town. The two men went to find Smith, which they did. A physical confrontation ensued, during which the sheriff's throat was cut. Sharp was able to use a firearm from the police vehicle to kill Smith in an act of fear and self-defense. Both Smith and Darby were declared dead at the scene.

For those who are not familiar with the story, Smith was suspected of the rapes and murders of Katie Castleman, Jane Feister, Carly Reed, Tim Bascom, Meredith Downs, and local student Diane Jensen.

It is also reported that, because, the death of Darby has left Burdensville without a sheriff, the state will provide a temporary fill-in pending the hire of a permanent replacement.

Donations for the victims' families are being received by the State Police in lieu of flowers.

∞

Scott closed the paper and folded it in half. He tossed it onto the chair next to him and took a long drink of his coffee, which Donna had just refilled. He was waiting to meet Denise; she hadn't been working due to her grief, and Scott had pretty much not left her side.

He heard the bell jingle on the café door and turned around. Denise was coming toward him. She looked better than she had looked. Her hair was combed and she had a little mascara on. Scott smiled when he saw her, and he stood up in greeting.

"You look like you're feeling better," he said.

Denise shrugged. "A little, I guess. I'm just relieved that it's all over."

"Me too." He sat next to her and put his arm around her. He gave her a gentle kiss and then turned back to his coffee.

Donna approached carrying a carafe of coffee. "Hey, Denise. It's so good to see you getting out. How are you feeling, dear?"

Denise took a breath. "I think about as good as could be expected."

Donna put the carafe down and embraced her friend. "Are you planning to come back to work?"

Denise shook her head. "At least, not in the near future."

"Well," Donna continued, "you know Dickie will let you back whenever you're ready."

Dickie popped his head through the window. "Hey!" he came through the kitchen's swinging doors, his arms outstretched. He took Denise in a bear hug. "How's my girl doin'?"

"I'm good, Dickie. Well, I'm better anyway," she replied. "I think I'm gonna make it."

"Well, with this guy by your side, I think you stand more than half a chance." He released Denise and gave Scott a hearty pat on the back and a smile.

Denise grinned at Scott, her eyes filled with affection. "Isn't he amazing? I don't know what I'd do without him."

"Where are you staying, hon?"

Denise turned her attention back to Dickie. "Right now, we're staying at the Morning Dew Motel, but that's only for a bit. Scott has decided to attend the academy so he can police this rat hole of a town. We'll be moving into Sheriff Darby's old place. I can't even imagine trying to go back to my house."

Dickie offered her a sympathetic nod. "Well, I better get back in the kitchen or all these people are gonna have my head." He gave the pair another firm slap on the back and disappeared through the swinging doors once again.

"All these people?" Donna and the pair turned around; the only other customers were the Harris sisters. "Dickie is gonna end up dying in that damn kitchen. Everyone is tickled about you going to the academy, Scott."

"Well, we all see a lot of potential in Burdensville," he replied. "I think, it's time someone started to act on it."

"Keep it up," Donna said, then she turned to Denise. "Now, you take care. We'll be seein' you around, okay?"

The two women hugged once more, and Donna went back to work. "Are you hungry?" Scott asked.

"Nah," she replied. "I had a bowl of soup before I came."

Scott stood then. "Well, I have all the business done I needed to do here in town. Are you ready to head back to the motel?"

Denise rose from her seat as well. "I'm ready to go anywhere you want to go."

Scott leaned forward and kissed her on her cute little nose. "I love you, you know."

"Ditto," she said as she planted a kiss on him as well.

Scott wrapped his arm over her shoulder and together they walked out of Dickie's café to the new car they had just bought. As they drove out toward Highway 16, they left the past behind them. It was time to head into the future.

R.W.K. Clark

EPILOGUE

Scott drove his cruiser up and down the narrow streets of Burdensville, making it a point to stop and visit with anyone who happened to be out and about. It was a warm, sunny day so there were quite a few. He loved to visit with the locals as much as he could.

He was looking forward to supper; Denise was making fried chicken and noodle salad, which was his favorite. He planned to have a tall, cold glass of her iced tea with his meal.

More than four years had passed so quickly. Denise had done him the honor of becoming his wife, and they had a handsome, smart little boy named Raymond. Raymond was four, and he was in preschool. He loved to ride his bike and play with his little friends. He was the spitting image of his mother, which made Scott happy. His heart swelled thinking about those two.

Denise was getting ready to have their second child any day. It was to be a boy, and they were going to name him Brian. She seemed to be nesting the last few days, so Scott thought the child would come very, very soon.

He pulled the cruiser into the driveway of their home, which used to be Darby's. He shut the ignition off, but sat there for a moment, his mind considering Darby. What a mess Burdensville had been in for a while after the sheriff was killed. Scott finally opened the door and climbed out of the car. He hated thinking about those days, but they were always with him, seared into his mind for good.

He slammed the car door shut, and that was when he heard the crying. Scott ran for the house as fast as he could. He flung open the front door to see his pregnant wife lying on the floor at the bottom of the stairs.

"What the heck?"

Denise was lying on the hard floor, heaving and pushing. She was ghostly white. Raymond was seated next to her, a stricken look on his face.

He turned to Scott. "Mommy fell down the stairs, Daddy. She fell hard."

Scott could see the blood between her legs. "Raymond, call Dr. Eddings. You know how; his number is on the fridge."

The boy ran to obey his father while Scott positioned himself between her legs and worked her yoga pants down. "It's going to be okay, Neece. I'm here now."

She looked at him through half closed eyes. Her breathing was shallow, and she was getting more and more pale by the second. She gave him a half-hearted smile and shook her head at him.

"You're going to be fine," he said once again. She was losing a lot of blood.

Raymond, "Did you call?"

"Yes, Daddy!" Raymond ran back into the room and knelt next to his mother. She began to push in earnest, but she didn't have the strength. It didn't matter; that baby was coming.

"Look, Daddy, the baby's head!" Raymond turned to his mother with excitement while Scott focused on delivering the child. "The baby's head, Mommy!"

Now she seemed to be fading. She smiled at Raymond while Scott worked, and in only another moment the child was born. Scott ripped his uniform shirt off as best as he could with one hand and wrapped the new baby in it.

"Look, Neece," he said to his wife with tears in his eyes. "He's perfect."

Denise turned to Raymond once more. "Raymond," she said weakly, "No matter what happens you protect your brother." With that, Denise was gone.

Raymond understood, and he made the silent promise: he would make sure nothing ever happened to baby Brian...

ENTREATY

My creativity is fueled by readers like you. If you enjoyed this novel, I implore you to please write a review, and share your experience on the retailer's website. The livelihood for authors is fully dependent on reviews, and I must say, it is the largest obstacle as a struggling author that I have encountered. Please tell a friend, tell a loved one about this read. With your help, I will be one step closer to overcoming this obstacle. In return, I thank you from the bottom of my heart, and greatly and deeply appreciate your time and effort.

Humbled, with gratitude,
R.W.K. Clark

ADDITIONALLY

Works by R.W.K. Clark

BROTHER'S KEEPER

ISBN-13: 978-1948312134 ISBN-10: 1948312131
ISBN-13: 978-0692744741 ISBN-10: 0692744746
ISBN-13: 978-1948312141 ISBN-10: 194831214X

Psychological Thriller

'Brother's Keeper' is my first psychological thriller, and it was simultaneously fun and difficult to write. It tells the story of Scott Sharp, a widowed traveler whose train makes a stop at the tiny town of Burdensville. Here, Scott tries to assist a waitress being harassed by a drunk and gets himself arrested, which results in pulling the stranger into the dark secrets the town holds, and the secrets won't let him go.

Writing this story was fun for a variety of reasons. It was off the beaten path compared to most books I write. The monster in this book is not a vampire, witch, or zombie; instead, the monster is an unknown man who is murdering women at night who pass through the town. Developing the character of the murderer was a good time; I wanted him to be dull, but intelligent; he needed to be needy, but in control in ways no one understood. He needed to have deep-seated issues that were in such a terrible knot that even those who might care about him didn't know how to sort them out.

Scott walks into Burdensville without the slightest idea what has been happening to this town. He is, utterly and completely, an innocent victim. When he first gets to the café and tries to protect the waitress from the town drunk, he is put under arrest by the sheriff, which is really the first sign that something is off in that town; even the other patrons in the restaurant keep their mouths closed when he implores them to tell the sheriff that he did nothing wrong. The whole place is off, and he can't seem to put his finger on what is happening around him. All Scott knows is that he's trapped in a jail cell waiting to see a judge that won't come for more than a week, but it is there that Scott himself will begin to unravel the goings-on in Burdensville for himself.

Of course, we cannot have a murder mystery without romance, even if it is slight. In the case of Brother's Keeper, I created a slow but sure relationship between Scott and the waitress he tried to save when he was arrested. In the beginning, she was aloof with him, but soon she is forced to take meals to the jail to feed Scott, and it is during this time the two get to know each other. Inevitably, they fall in love, but not before the killer puts her own sanity to the test.

Sheriff Robert Darby is keeping the most secrets in this town, as readers will discover. I chose the sheriff for this role because none of what happens in the book would be possible without the authority that his badge permits him to have. Now, some may say that the storyline in regard to him is somewhat flaky or unrealistic. I would have to tell those readers that this is fiction. The beauty of fiction is exactly what I did in the case of Sheriff Darby and his unutterable secrets.

I tried to put a bit of everything in this book: Old lady hen twins who are the gossipers of the town; Dickie, the café owner, who has great fatherly affection for Denise, and who has seen some of the craziness Burdensville truly has to offer. The town drunk, who is also mentally challenged and basically faces life alone except for the help of the sheriff; he is essential to the novel, in all of its insanity and desperation.

To put things in a nutshell for my readers, there is a past history that the sheriff is actively covering up; he is doing this for more reasons than I can explain here, but his secrets are vile, shameful, and have instilled a sense of obligation in Sheriff Darby that he can never silence. It is, quite literally, a huge burden for him, but he carries these things, and acts upon them, out of the best interest of the townsfolk as a whole, not to mention himself. Readers may feel like Sheriff Darby is something of a bad guy, but I cannot express enough that the things he does which seem so wrong are committed out of a pure heart, a heart that is trying to make things right in a situation where they will never, ever be right again. He is not the guy to hate here, though throughout the pages it clearly seems that way. The reality is, Sheriff Darby is as much of a victim as all of those who have been murdered on the outskirts of the town.

I wanted people to really be in Burdensville while they read this. I also wanted readers to get a very specific feel for the town; Mayberry without a shower. I did my best to convey the gloom of the constant shadows that seem to hang over the place, even when the sun was shining. I also wanted to make it clear that Sheriff Darby wasn't the only one feeling obligation; the entire town does. That's more or less what happens in small-town life and, evil or not, Burdensville is no different.

PASSING THROUGH

ISBN-10: 1948312018 ISBN-13: 978-1948312011
ISBN-10: 1948312093 ISBN-13: 978-1948312097
ISBN-10: 1948312107 ISBN-13: 978-1948312103
ISBN-10: 1948312115 ISBN-13: 978-1948312110

Psychological Thriller

I believe that writers and novelists, as in any profession, change and grow over the timespan that they work and produce. Any of my readers and fans who are familiar with my books and the 'genres' they are 'classified' under are able to recognize the point I am making. Authors' characters get more detailed and personal; descriptions get a bit more intense, as do emotional scenes of any kind. I have also found, for myself, that with each and every book I put out, I seem to get a bit more 'guts' about what I am willing to put down on paper. For instance, I'll admit it, in the beginning, writing a detailed love scene was something I dreaded, but I do much better now, and I'm getting much more comfortable, with experience, in that particular area. This, of course, is just one example.

'Passing Through' is my latest release, and it is the third book I have written that I would call a psychological thriller. The first was 'Brother's Keeper', and when I wrote that I thought it was a bit much. 'Passing Through' is on an entirely different level, however, not just in its depth and explicitness. Now, I realize that there will be fans out there who will love this book; perhaps it will surprise them, and they will find it will be just what they were waiting for from me. Others, though, are going to despise it.

'Passing Through' was very difficult for me to write for a number of reasons, but there were two in particular that took a toll on me. First, I have had close personal experience and interactions in passing with violent criminals, and their minds and ways of thinking are ugly and burdensome; they are not people you want to make regular friends of. To put these things into words and make people understand was, well, exhausting.

I also found myself quite beaten up after writing each and every violent part. I didn't want the parts to be mild, because the character of Elliot Keller was a horrible, horrible man. It thrilled him to do the things he did to people to the point that the only motivation he had for escaping prison was to have a chance to indulge in his deviant behavior yet once more in his life. Some of the visuals I got, which are what prompt what I write, made me sick, and more than once, I had to step away and breathe.

Now, let's talk about Keller a bit better. Initially, I wrote his character with little to no explanation as to why he was the killer that he was. It didn't matter at first; to me, he was just a bad man, an animal. Many murderers never suffer wrong at the hands of another, yet they choose to harm others over and over, for no other reason than they like it and it's fun.

I changed this. The reason I began to explain a bit about what made Elliot what he was is simple: I had to show readers the ripple effect, that can literally last for centuries, when this type of violence is bestowed by one on another. What happened to Keller, Keller did to others, and it would not stop there… it would never stop. I didn't go into his past to provoke pity or compassion. He is nothing more than a rabid animal, and his actions clearly demonstrate that. With that being said, by the end of the book, you will understand what I mean, and you will still hate him all the more.

Thompson Trails, Virginia is yet another fictional town full of ignorant, innocent unawares that have no idea what is about to hit them. I love to develop these little burgs, and I enjoy creating the people who live blissfully within their boundaries. I grow to love many of the characters, no matter how brief their appearances; as readers know, authors kill people off, no matter their age or how good of a person they are. This happens a lot in Thompson Trails, and I grieved each death. But in reality, killers don't flip coins, and they don't pick and choose. Bad things happen, and they always seem to happen to good people.

Finally, I would like to touch base briefly on Rick and Donna Welk, the owners of the cabin resort, but mostly I want to focus on Donna. Donna and Rick have suffered the loss of a pregnancy, which spurred them to move and buy the cabins. On the outside, Donna is soft, kind, generous, a good wife, and wouldn't hurt a fly. She is hurting that she cannot have a child, and she is simply trying to build a new, happy life around this reality. I believe that readers are going to be surprised by the fiber this little woman is made of, and I think they will be furious at the outcome Keller causes her and the man she loves.

For those of you who are lovers of horror, well, here you go. I hope you enjoy it. I also hope it makes you as sick as it makes me, because it is that horror and sickness that makes us face the harsh realities of life and keeps us on our toes. I didn't write this and then roll it in sugar because it isn't candy; it is a jagged little pill that will slice your throat straight open if you swallow too fast. Believe me, when I say, it is not for children. Best to give fair warning; I wrote this in a manner that it would leave some kind of mark. Hopefully, the mark is a good one.

So, sit down with the lights on and enjoy the terror that is Elliot Keller in 'Passing Through'.

BOX OFFICE BUTCHER

ISBN-10: 0997876751 ISBN-13: 978-0997876758

Psychological Thriller

Box Office Butcher is a psychological thriller murder mystery about a killer who is murdering people in an identical manner as that which is done in a new hit slasher flick. While the premise is similar to that of the popular 'Scream' franchise, readers will find that I have written this in a manner that is actually much different, making it unique in almost every aspect. The bottom line, however, is the same: There is a lunatic killing people out there, and he has to be stopped.

Dubbed 'The Box-Office Butcher' by the press, the killer is committing a couple of killings every weekend, and he isn't doing this in a specific area; he's moving around. This results in Detective Kevin Harmes, of the Los Angeles Police Department, scrambling from here to there and back again to try and keep up. Fortunately, this seasoned cop has some pretty spot-on suspicions of his own. Regardless of this fact, 'The Butcher' manages to keep him on his toes, and miserably so, with the sick game he is playing.

It is important to understand that the killer has a vendetta, and it is very necessary to accomplish it. For him, these murders are rooted in a history of abuse and rage, and he feels the compelling need to take care of the issue, which he has carried around with him his entire life. It is more than simply killing because he's a sicko, or because it's fun, though these are true as well. His actions are essentially a way to make right a past that has, unbeknownst to him, destroyed him from the inside out.

Keep in mind that none of the 'copycat' killings are identical to the one from the film which they are meant to emulate. The Butcher doesn't have the kind of power it would take to make his victims cooperate with a scripted film and still enjoy the spontaneity and horror he is set on sparking and enjoying. With this being said, he is a careful planner, spending both time and money to get the real-life murders as close to the ones on film as he possibly can, and he comes terrifyingly close each time.

The Butcher is a man of means, and this becomes obvious by his ability to move so freely from city to city; obviously, he isn't broke or lacking finances of some kind. This is a point which Detective Harmes picks up on and is vital to his investigation. Unfortunately, the suspects that are on his list all fall into this category at one level or another, so he must do the footwork to weed them out.

The Butcher is a very sick man, and it was important to drive this home through a variety of methods. I wrote about him watching the scenes over and over again, which he was preparing to emulate, even though it was obvious he knew them like the back of his hand. I also added an element of sexual stimulation when he watched, as an added bonus pointing to his psychosis.

The hardest part of this work, for me, was keeping the real killer's identity from being given away during the investigation. It was difficult to give some hints here and there while still shining the spotlight on another, as a distraction. There was a fine line here that couldn't be crossed, at least, not immediately, and it was like a balancing act to walk that line. It helped to have The Butcher intentionally raising suspicion on other suspects who could reasonably be the killer that he actually was.

Why is Kevin Harmes so obsessed? Because he believes that every wrong turn he has taken, and each incorrect assumption he has made, is being orchestrated by The Butcher, and this enrages him. As an experienced detective, the fact that a criminal like The Butcher knows that Harmes will buy his bluff and veer off in another direction is bothersome, to say the least. He almost takes this as an assault on his policing ability. Sure, people are dying, but for Harmes, that's just the tip of the iceberg. The Butcher is also basically making fun of the cops, running them around from city to city in confusion, like small children trying to catch a balloon filled with helium, but is always out of reach.

As can be expected, as the story goes on, Harmes finds little tidbits here and there which begin to clear the fog covering The Butcher's identity. Everything begins to make sense, and sure enough, the killer is someone who has been on his suspect list all along. The person has misdirected and lied to the point that it should have been obvious from the beginning. By the time Harmes is ready to nab the guy, he finds that he isn't a step ahead at all; rather, The Butcher already has a plan for this, as well, and it includes Kevin Harmes.

Box Office Butcher, with all difficulties aside, was a fun novel to write. The murder mystery genre label which it falls under afforded me much freedom; I just had to sort my way through what was believable and what would appear to be smoke and mirrors to the reader. I had to reconcile the two to each other without giving away The Butcher's identity too quickly, and hopefully, I accomplished this properly. I also had a lot of fun with The Butcher's past, though it was horrid. The abuse the guy went through at the hands of his own twisted, sick mother are enough to cause anyone to almost understand how someone could go to the kinds of extremes that this killer did.

BLOOD FEATHER AWAKENS

ISBN-10: 0692734082 ISBN-13: 978-0692734087

Crime Thriller

Of all the books I have penned, 'Blood Feather Awakens' was one of the most fun for me. It tells the story of Sam Daniels, a wildlife photographer who, while on assignment in the Amazon jungle, encounters a breathtakingly beautiful but horribly deadly, prehistoric bird. Sam witnesses the bloody killing of his guide but manages to snap a couple of grainy photographs, which he takes to an ornithologist at the University of Washington for identification. That is just the beginning of the tale; Sam and the beautiful Dr. Kate Beck, accompanied by three guides and tailed by a couple of fame-seeking paleontologists, venture back to the jungle to find, and hopefully capture, the murderous creature.

Why was this book so much fun to write? I would have to attribute it simply to the imagination involved in it. From Sam's first encounter with the bird, all the way to its capture and return to the States, I found it was a subject I could really do anything with, if I so chose. I wanted to make the time in the jungle both horrifying, thanks to the evasive bird, and romantic, due to the blossoming romance between Kate and Sam. I also wanted it to be bloody, because let's face it: If a massive prehistoric bird were to attack, well, it would be nothing but bloody.

I also thrived on creating realistic relationships between all of the people. For instance, even though Sam and Kate are in the company of jungle guides, all of them are in this terrible situation together. It was imperative that they talk and laugh, that they come to trust and depend on each other in a way that simply would not take place on a normal jungle tour. Everyone is frightened, but they are also eager. The tour guides are also angry that one of their own has been killed, and they want the threat removed before anyone else is harmed. Sam and Kate want the bird captured and studied; they want to keep it safe while ensuring the safety of the world.

But then we have the two paleontologists, Dr. Harold Kreiger and Dr. Roy Hastings. These two men work at the University of Washington, just as Kate does. Since they are colleagues of hers, she takes Sam to see them when he brings her the photograph of the bird and recognizes it as 'prehistoric' in nature. But, just as she fears, these two begin to see how beating Kate and Sam to the punch will make them famous, and these two men try to get to the creature and locate it before Sam and Kate. This turns out bad for Kreiger and Hastings, but I have to admit, it was more than a pleasure to create the demise these two selfish men deserved.

I wanted the truth about how dangerous this thing was in my own mind to be clearly conveyed; this bird can think, reason, and use logic. The humans which pursue it may outsmart it and capture it, but all it needs is a little time to sort things out and find a way to appease its own bloodthirsty nature. This thing was never meant to be captured; after all, it survived a meteor hitting the Earth millions of years ago, and it has managed to continue its species for the sole reason that 'life will find a way'. The determination that was shown to simply survive needed to clearly reflect its ability to destroy, as well. I believe that I portrayed all of this clearly and concisely, especially at the very end.

So, what is 'Blood Feather'? To put it simply, the creature is, indeed, a bird, but it is prehistoric, related to the 'archaeopteryx' but much larger. In my mind, when humans discover the bones of prehistoric animals, all we really can do is guess as to what their real appearance would have been like. Now, perhaps they did look like that, but I venture to say that it is likely we are off a bit in our assumptions. I did nothing more than to create my own creature, in my own mind. Some of its physical traits are the same, some are different. This is the reason Kate and the paleontologists are uncertain of what it is: They are stuck with an assumed picture in their overly-educated minds.

But exactly what Blood Feather is, is not important. The bottom line is that it's a killer. It lives on flesh and blood, and it gets pleasure from the hunt and chase. It is airborne, so there really is no escape, and it has the ability to somewhat hypnotize its prey with its eerily human eyes. It is meant to confuse and terrify, which is precisely what I designed it for. Its beauty is deceptive;

it will lure you in and then end your life. To be honest, this was the most fun for me: Writing about presumptuous humans who are scrambling around out of their element, trying to get the best of nature's perfect killing machine.

I truly hope readers are as entertained by this story as I was by writing it. I tried to keep it light and simple without compromising fear or blood. I also wanted to tell a story that would keep the reader turning pages. I think that those who read this fun and frightening story will appreciate it in the end, for what I intended it to be.

SHATTERED DREAMS

ISBN-10: 0997876719 ISBN-13: 978-0997876710

Crime Thriller

When I sat down to write 'Shattered Dreams', I did it with one purpose in mind, and it was a very simple purpose: To tell a story. It isn't like my other novels in that it is in no way 'supernatural' or 'psychological'; it is just the tale of a man with dreams who brought them to life, only to have them ripped away from him in the most desperate and unfair way possible. It is something that could really happen; there are no zombies or vampires, and there are no magical formulas being produced. Only a man, his dream, and the enemy who hates him.

So, let me begin with my main character, Jimmy O'Brien. Jimmy is a good boy from the beginning, the offspring of a loser Irish father and devoted Italian mother. From as far back as Jimmy can remember, he has had a single dream: To be a cop, and to fight the bad guys. He makes all the right choices, even from youth, to obtain his goal; he even goes the extra mile on more than one occasion.

Let's begin at the start, or as close to it as effectively possible. Jimmy's mother raises him alone, thanks to his father running off with another. The man had it all at one point: A wife, a son, and a good job. But rather than acting according to his priorities, he not only cheats and leaves, but he also resorts to criminal behavior that includes beating up the woman he left his wife for. Jimmy despises this behavior, even going so far as to refuse to call his father 'dad'. Along with television cop shows, it is this behavior that dictates Jimmy's hatred toward those who harm others in any criminal way.

But in his mother, Jimmy has a person who would go to the ends of the Earth for her son to be happy and well provided for. She supports him in all of his ventures, and even though she is afraid for his safety, she also backs him in his pursuit of a police career. Luciana O'Brien is a wonderful, moral woman who deserves to have something good happen to her in her life.

Jimmy has several other people who support him, from friends to the chief of his hometown police department, Matias Garcia. Over the years, all the right doors open at the right times, and Jimmy, true to his form, always walks straight through each and every one of them. Soon, he is a grown man with a job working as a real police officer, and he is nearing his goal of becoming chief for the entire department. He has a beautiful fiancé, and everything is coming together just as he had always planned.

But when an old school rival of Jimmy's comes back into the picture as a runner for the Mexican cartel, things take a terrible turn. All of his dreams are now being threatened, and before he knows it, corruption in the department is plotting to steal the dreams he has held so dear to his heart, taking everything and everyone he loves as well.

What is the point of this book? As the writer, I would have to firmly say that the point is: Nothing ever goes as planned, and more often than not, our hearts are broken terribly. Jimmy is innocent, quite literally, in this story, but by the end of the book, he is suffering consequences which only the evil should have to endure. Why? Because, to put it as simply as possible, that's life.

The things which happen to Jimmy at the hands of others are much less impactful if the reader doesn't have a firm grasp on who this young man is, morally speaking. This is someone who would rather die than do harm to another. This is someone who really couldn't tell a lie if he wanted to. Jimmy is trustworthy, soft-hearted, compassionate, and bent on doing the right thing. His every action is motivated by a solid desire to operate out of integrity, and nothing else.

All of his hardship towards the end stems from a toxic friendship he had in the first grade with a boy named Kevin Marshall. Kevin is a bad seed, through and through. When the boy gets caught for stealing from a classmate, Jimmy knows, without a doubt, that he cannot continue their friendship. But it is Kevin Marshall who Jimmy must confront in high school for dealing drugs, and it is Kevin Marshall who sparks the chain of events in adulthood which ultimately prove to be Jimmy's destruction. The point? The past will come back to haunt you, even if you weren't the one doing the haunting in the first place.

As far as Jimmy is concerned, he is a character that I have a certain amount of love for, in a literal way. I admire the man I created, and as I created his life and heartaches, I hurt for him. I found myself infuriated with the bad guys I put in his life, but at the same time, I realized I wasn't willing to bail him out of his injustices. This is the life I created for Henry James O'Brien, and this is his destiny, unfortunately.

I think readers will like this book, but not because it is frightening or abstract. Readers will enjoy it because of the level of reality they will find in its pages. I also think they will feel the same way about Jimmy that I do, and I believe they will experience anger at the unfairness that goes on in his life. In the end, 'Shattered Dreams' is a highly relatable story for anyone who decides to venture into its pages.

REQUIEM FOR THE CAGED

ISBN-10: 1948312026 ISBN-13: 978-1948312028

Romantic Suspense

Coming from the perspective of someone who creates, I believe I can say with confidence that my new book, 'Requiem for the Caged', may not be for everyone. I knew this from the start, and even as I sat down to write it, I simply wanted to tell a story I hadn't told before, and it happened to fall into a far different category than my fans are used to.

First of all, this particular story has nothing to do with the undead, or bloodsuckers of any kind. It has nothing to do with aliens, or youth potions, or tainted futuristic seas. It is a love story, pure and simple. Unconventional? Of course. But love is never really conventional in any way, now is it? So, why should it be conventional in the pages of a book?

First, I would like to begin by discussing the premise. Jason Brandtley is a good young man. He has just returned from being a prisoner of war overseas and is facing the impending death of his mother. He is a young man with a gentle spirit and full of integrity, but he has suffered many recent traumas, and with his mother being sick, they really aren't over yet. But that doesn't change the fact that his heart and soul are clean, and the motives of his heart are always based on his desire to do the right thing and help.

After his mother dies, Jason inherits the family sheep ranch, but he is having to run operations on his own. Lonely and depressed, Jason longs for a wife to share his life with. He is eager, and he is willing to do what it takes to find a good woman to walk by his side.

Andrea is a waitress who lives and works in Cheyenne, about thirty minutes away. He meets her while having lunch in the park one day, and Jason is stricken with her immediately. But Andrea is a polar opposite to Jason, as readers will see. Unlike Jason, a much-loved only child, Andrea comes from a family that is harsh and uncaring; her mother has essentially turned her back on the girl, forcing her to be strong and emotionally detached when it comes to life. The pair does have one thing in common, however: they both have suffered heartbreak several times at the hands of love interests. The thing that sets them apart is how they have chosen to respond to the pain. While Jason is able to somewhat put it behind him, Andrea's every action and reaction is based on the abuse she has suffered from men.

Jason doesn't know this, and he begins to pursue her, only to be shot down in flames and actually assaulted by her ex for his efforts. This assault sends the ex-POW over the edge, and he determines to teach Andrea a lesson. He builds a cage in his basement for her, abducts her, and refuses her release until she changes her ways.

That is as strange as this novel gets, however. It is here that the two, who are now in each other's constant company, begin to get to know one another. They begin to realize that everyone suffers heartache, but it is never a reason to re-inflict. They also begin to see each other differently in this light, and inevitably, love begins to grow.

Now, there is no torture or murder involved in this novel. The desire of Jason's heart is to genuinely help Andrea, even though he has gone to a terrifying and unacceptable length to do so. Andrea is only initially frightened of harm; she is soon convinced he couldn't hurt her if he wanted to, and this realization is the turning point in their relationship.

Why did I decide to write such a story, especially when most of my works are thrillers? Well, I would have to say that, in my opinion and from my experience, love can be the strangest and scariest thing of all. I wanted to try romantic suspense and see how two people from totally different backgrounds react to each other's pain. I wanted to play with the idea that, even if someone 'flips their lid', so to speak, they can still love and be loved. I also wanted to express the deep importance of communication in learning to love and accept one another for all that each of us is. This involves understanding that each of us is made up of all of our happiness and heartaches. Each laugh and every tear are what we consist of. Most of the time, these things can cause us to act in a manner that is repulsive or frightening, or painful, to those around us, just like in the cases of both Jason and Andrea. But these things can also be overcome if the other is willing to look at the whole person instead of just the ugly parts. That is where the beauty of love comes in.

Yes, Dear Readers, this is what you may label a 'romance' or 'love story', and that may be a jagged pill for some of you to swallow coming from me. But the fact is, love is just as much a part of life as our fear of the monster in the closet, or the stalker outside the window. It is even more a part of life than any of these because it is the basis for our sanity and survival.

It is my sincere hope that you all enjoy this book for what it is: A simple, yet complicated, tale of two people who find love in the most unlikely of places. It is the story about cages, and how all of us live in them in one way or another. Most of all, it is about acceptance of the person trapped in the cage across from yours.

OUT TO SEA

ISBN-10: 099787676X ISBN-13: 978-0997876765

Romantic Suspense

'Out to Sea' was a project that I had to walk a fine line with. I intended for it to be a work with a very pertinent message, while forming a bond between star-crossed teen lovers that is destined to end with the cruise they were on. With the state of the future world in shambles, it was somewhat difficult to know when and where romance was truly appropriate; after all, the planet is dying before the eyes of the main characters, and they are literally watching everyone basically celebrate it. It's the sort of thing that can ruin the mood.

The basic plot of the book revolves around a chemical spill which has made all the water on Earth poisonous, even to the touch. Man has created an electrolyte-based alternative for drinking, and other methods which are less than natural are used for bathing, swimming, etc. The fact of the matter is that the end will come as a direct result of this, and most everyone is painfully aware that the future is dark and grim.

There are those, however, who have found a way to exploit the situation. The spill has made the appearance of the water indescribably gorgeous, even entrancing, to a certain level. People purchase atrociously priced luxury cruises for the sole purpose of gawking at the lifeless seas, and they seem to have no care for what the façade of beauty they are looking at really means. It is truly a horrible thing, and I wanted the level of depravity and complacency to which human beings stoop to be stark and ugly.

Tripp Young is my main character on this ocean voyage. As the only son of wealthy parents, he is expected to go on these yearly excursions with them. They are two of the countless who have bought into the horrible exploitation of the planet's impending death, and they seem blind to the reality of it all. To them, and all others like them, it is an amusement park ride, of sorts.

But Tripp is neither ignorant nor calloused to what is taking place. He looks at his existence as taking place in two categories: Before the Spill, and After the Spill, and the planets in both are very different places indeed. For a seventeen-year-old, he is very in touch with logic and sense, as well as the brokenhearted emotion he nurses for the world that was once lush with grass and other plant life; a world where you could jump in a river and swim. Tripp had to be angry, but I also knew it had to be a righteous, self-controlled anger, an anger with a purpose.

While on this joke of a cruise, Tripp meets Heidi Collins, and is instantly smitten with the smart, petite environmentally conscious redhead. Never having a real girlfriend before, he easily becomes consumed with spending as much time together while on the water as they can, and her feelings are the same. Together, they witness some pretty horrific things, which can all be attributed to the tainted sea that surrounds them. It pulls them closer and closer as the days pass.

One such scene involves a child who goes missing during the cruise. The ship's staff searches high and low for her, to no avail. Tripp, Heidi, and two of their friends watch and listen in disgusted awe as the ship continues on the water, because the show must go on. Finally, the kids decide to look for the girl themselves, on the sly.

This is one tragedy that takes place aboard the ship. It was important to convey the state of mind of those who enjoyed what the spill had done; depraved indifference and selfishness filled their souls. I contemplated the accomplishment, though it may have seemed overly dramatic in manner, at times.

As for Tripp and Heidi's love, it was doomed from the start; in my mind, this was to be a sad tale of not only the results of man's wreaking havoc on Mother Earth, but of unrequited love. These two kids genuinely love each other, and they swear to be together again. Deep inside, they both know they will not, but it is something they are not willing to even consider. I wanted the reader to feel the hopelessness and emptiness they felt at the thought of the day they would say goodbye, and I truly hope I managed to get that done. I wanted their interactions to be intensely emotional and painful, so they could be tangible to the person with the book.

To put it simply, 'Out to Sea' is an environmentally conscious romantic suspense that has no blissful ending, but it tells a story, and it teaches a lesson. It may not feel good, but lessons rarely do. I think by the end of this book, whether the reader loves it or hates it, they will never forget it. I wrote it to be the kind of story that sticks, even if it isn't popular for the particular content or level of fiction. With that being said, this is one of my personal favorites as a writer, and it had an impact on me that my other works haven't. It may be a fiction novel, but the pain and despair I put in the pages was anything but a fairy tale; I'm confident the emotion will help get the message across loud and clear.

PASSAGE OF TIME

ISBN-10: 0997876727 ISBN-13: 978-0997876727

Romantic Suspense

'Passage of Time' is actually one of my personal favorites, and I hope you enjoy reading it as much as I enjoyed writing it.

This was never intended to be a thriller novel; it just barely makes it into the science fiction realm, only doing so because of the 'fountain of youth' premise. Mostly, this book is a romantic suspense, but it is also a story of time wasted in an effort to live forever. It is a tale which has been shaped by years of regret and sadness, which are only realized at the very end.

Calvin Cooper is a man with a mission. A scientist, both by trade and by nature, Calvin wants to help others look and feel younger. Early on, he meets Elaina, the woman destined to be the love of his life and his eternal companion. Together, Calvin believes they will conquer the world. With her patience, he will come up with the end-all, be-all solution, and then they will be together forever, literally.

There is no end to Elaina's loyalty or patience. It was important to create in her, a character who is totally devoted, no matter what she may face with her man. Throughout their lives, and his work, she is his rock, and his love for her knows no bounds. Unfortunately, she is also the only one who looks at things realistically, and Calvin is destined to learn one of the most painful lessons of his life through her: People were never meant to live forever.

One situation the two endure together involves an animal rights activist group who has targeted Calvin, believing that his work involves harming animals. But even through this scary incident in their lives, Elaina is his strong tower and primary support, and his love for her grows.

Over time, Calvin begins to make progress with his formula, and while his wife is extremely supportive when it comes to meeting his goals, she is not one who believes that human beings should endure indefinitely. But she is the kind of woman who will ignore her own beliefs if it means backing up the man she loves. Calvin, however, is oblivious to all of this. The years pass, and more progress is made. As he considers all the time he has spent focusing on his work, he tries to push the guilt aside that he feels for putting poor Elaina on the back burner. He reassures himself that when the formula is perfected, the two of them will enjoy eternity in each other's arms.

Ralph Gordon is another character who was necessary to the lesson Calvin is set to learn. Ralph comes on as Calvin's assistant, and they too end up forging an unbreakable friendship. He, like Elaina, is dedicated, and he truly cares about the person who is doing all the work. But Ralph just wants to live his days out in peace; living forever isn't even remotely attractive to him. Calvin seems to be stuck in a huge lack of understanding; both Ralph and Elaina could spell things out for him, but his genius has stolen his ability to look at things from the heart. Without Ralph, Calvin would likely just consider that Elaina's opinions are formed because she is something of an emotional woman.

Another character who tries to get the point across, in a much more subdued manner, is Noah Carter, the sick old man who first owned Maddie, the horse. But when given the option to continue on, permanently, in his newfound youth, Noah gratefully refuses, explaining his stance clearly and concisely. This is yet another example of Calvin being so blinded by his dreams that he has become numb to life's realities; he has no grasp whatsoever on why these people would refuse, nor is he able to consider giving up.

Calvin Cooper is, in a sense, every man. Anyone with any level of personal accountability or love in their heart wants to give the world to those who are the objects of his affection. If that man is able to cause his wife to live forever, he would, as would Calvin. But Calvin has lost touch with the very things that make us all human, and in his effort to work literal miracles, he allows his entire life to pass him by. It isn't until he comes to the point of being surrounded in his success while in utter isolation that Calvin begins to understand what he gave up for a dream that was never meant to become a reality.

Yes, I wrote 'Passage of Time' to be a love story. I wrote it with the intent of making readers feel the love between Calvin and Elaina in a very tangible sense, and

I hope I succeeded in that goal. But above and beyond that, this book was meant to make the reader consider who they have to love, and whether or not they are doing all that they can to demonstrate that love during the limited time they have. As we all know, there is no secret potion, no 'ElainaYouth' to consume that will give us countless years to revel in the gift of life. What each of us has, all that we have, is the here and now that ultimately makes up that thing we call 'today'.

So, in consideration of the above, I believe that mature readers will find 'Passage of Time' to be compelling and thought-provoking. I believe it will stimulate a spirit of gratefulness, when allowed, and I also believe it will leave readers with the simple satisfaction of having read a good book. In the end, that is the purpose of fiction, after all, and 'Passage of Time' is no exception.

DEAD ON THE WATER

ISBN-10: 0997876700 ISBN-13: 978-0997876703
ISBN-10: 1948312905 ISBN-13: 978-1948312905
ISBN-10: 1948312921 ISBN-13: 978-1948312929
ISBN-10: 194831293X ISBN-13: 978-1948312936

Zombie Thriller

This is another zombie contribution which I put a bit of a spin on. 'Dead on the Water' chronicles the story of a Fantasy Lines cruise ship which has a passenger who got bit by a dog during a shopping spree with her parents in Belize. Not knowing that the dog is carrying a terrible, zombie-making virus, the bite-victim re-boards the ship, and it returns to the vast ocean. Soon, the entire vessel is overrun with zombies, and those who have not been infected are fighting for their lives in the middle of the sea.

The first thing I would like to say about this particular book is that I allowed the zombies to be able to think, speak, and function, but they are the undead, nevertheless. The leader of the zombie pack, Captain James McElroy, even continues to be the leader in death that he was in life, and his plan is to not only take over the entire ship, but to get to land and carry on spreading the vile sickness when they dock in Houston.

This is a fast-paced book; once the action starts, it is pretty much non-stop. Being on a cruise ship, those who are still normal have very limited resources or means of escape. The ship has approximately three-thousand zombies trying to get to the last remaining survivors, so most of the ship's staff that are still alive are essentially barricaded into one part of the ship or another, including the bridge and a fitness center. They are desperate, with no weapons and no way to get off the ship without guaranteeing their own demise.

While it is about zombies, and there are several very graphic scenes, I do not believe it is necessarily a scary book. I tried to use dialogue in a surreal manner, especially coming from the monsters, in an effort to show the craziness and terrifying truth about the situation, but I didn't want it to be too heavy. My vision was simply to relate the hopelessness of the situation without making the book burdensome to read; I wanted it to be on the 'lighter' side, if possible.

Now, I presented a couple of different situations in the book. The primary one takes place on the ship; the second is happening at a shady lab in Belize, where the girl was bitten by a dog in the alley. This lab is sort of an underground operation run by a somewhat 'mad' scientist and his assistant, Bruce Ward; the good doctor relocated after the States stopped his experimentation. The long and short of it is that this lab has gone haywire, and its infected rats are beginning to run rampant. The CDC tries to gain control of this situation, which is sort of a side-line story to give you, the reader, a bit of hope that this craziness will be contained. I should warn you, especially my new readers: Don't get your hopes up. I find it difficult to imagine happy endings when it comes to the genres I write in, and I find it much easier to be horribly realistic.

But let's face it, I write about completely unrealistic stuff. What I'm trying to say is, the glory of fiction is in its falseness, but the impact of fiction is found in its painful reality. If a zombie apocalypse really happened, would the ending really be a good one? I think not; it would be hopeless and desperate, and that is the painful reality of this book.

Speaking of hope, let's talk about George Meade, Captain McElroy's assistant. So, we have the CDC battling things on land, but those still living on the ship are literally fighting a losing battle; they are fish in a barrel. If the zombies reach land, there will be a literal outbreak, and nothing the CDC is doing in Belize will matter. I allow George to escape in a lifeboat because someone on that damn cruise ship has to be smart enough to get away and get help. Pretty daunting task, don't you think? To reach the docking point before the ship, baking in the sun with no water, and having been through a terribly traumatic and unbelievable experience? Well, all I have to say about his success or failure is, you'll just have to see.

On another topic, I didn't get too deep with any of the characters as far as their personal appearance or personalities. There are many characters in 'Dead on the Water'; only a few hold the limelight, and none for very long; ultimately, it is 'every man for himself'.

So, as far as my second zombie tale goes, I hope you enjoy it. It's a little lighter than you might expect, but it is fast-paced, and you'll find plenty of gruesome scenes.

'Dead on the Water' is an easy and entertaining read. I hope you'll check out this book, and have fun reading it, too!

PERMANENT INK

ISBN-10: 0997876735 ISBN-13: 978-0997876734

Zombie Thriller

I wrote 'Permanent Ink' with mostly one message to convey: The price of greed can be astronomical, and most often, it is horribly destructive.

This is the story of a stationers' company that is on the brink of bankruptcy, but they have an ace in the hole: A new ink that appears almost holographic once it is on paper. Knowing that the kids will love it, Aspen Stationers' pushes for quick release of the pens developed to dispense the ink, wanting it available for public purchase before the school year starts. But the executives at Aspen have a secret: In the lab, the ink has had an adverse effect on rats, causing them to attack each other to the death, then bringing them back to life more violent and bloodthirsty than ever. Because this only happens when the ink is still wet, Aspen has convinced themselves that the world will be safe, and consumers will be none the wiser.

In an effort to show how widespread the destruction is, I scattered the storyline around a bit: One particular incident involving the ink takes place in a hospital in Thornton, Colorado. Another, in Aspen, where the company is located, and finally Monte Vista. The outbreak is taking place in the suburbs, but the local government is trying to figure things out, and has even called in the CDC. The catastrophe has even reached other areas, but for the sake of the story, I have kept the text limited to areas in Colorado.

First, let's look at the outbreak at the hospital. When a young girl gets the ink in a scrape, she is soon terribly ill. Her mother rushes her to the hospital to be seen, and the child is admitted. Even though she is exhibiting strange, and even violent, behavior, her mother is driven to comfort her, which leads to an attack. Before anyone even understands what is taking place, the 'zombie' sickness has spread like wildfire, and both patients and employees of the health care center are forced to fight for their lives. A pair of physicians are beginning to figure things out, slowly but surely, but will they solve the problem before it's too late?

The hospital scenes are fast-paced; it is chaos there, and the panic the characters are feeling should be tangible. I did the best I could to convey this, without giving too much hope to the situation, because frankly, I felt the situation in Thornton was fairly close to being hopeless.

In the situation with Aspen Stationers' scientist, Randy Carstens, he is fully aware of the potential for disaster, and he is sickened by the complacency of the executives in charge. Randy manages to get himself fired, but that doesn't keep him from returning and trying to stop the ball, which has already been set rolling. While there, the company's CEO, Roger McGinley, falls victim to the zombie rats while trying to force Randy to comply at gunpoint. Fortunately, Randy is able to escape and notify Aspen Police, but by the time they understand what is happening, they have a pretty big mess on their hands.

Which takes us to Brian Olson, a soon-to-be ninth grader at Monte Vista High School. Brian's single mother couldn't afford to buy him the expensive pen, but his best friend Caleb comes through. Brian tests the ink, which is said to smudge easily, with a finger. Unfortunately, he has a papercut, and the ink gets into his bloodstream. Overnight, the boy has died and becomes one of the bloodthirsty undead; his poor, unsuspecting mother is his first victim. Soon, the town is pretty much on lockdown, and the petrified people of Monte Vista are waiting for the CDC to come and save the day.

'Permanent Ink' is a zombie story, plain and simple, filled with the flesh-eating monsters that are all the rage at the current time. It is meant to gross readers out, to a certain extent, but mostly, with all of the chaotic scenes aside, I wanted to really convey a message. Corporate greed is the catalyst behind this horrible outbreak, wreaking havoc on unsuspecting consumers who have been blindsided by their timely marketing tactics. The worst part is, Aspen Stationers' is more than suspicious of the potential for damage that the ink has; they know full well what it can do, and they just don't care. This type of manipulation takes place every day in our world, with results just as destructive, only slower and less obvious. This truth is really what is behind the message in this book.

Of course, things have to be cleared up, and solutions must be found so life can go on. But as I mentioned earlier, I neither saw nor felt any positive resolution to this particular story, and as a writer, I had to struggle to make a way for the sun to rise on these towns again, with hope. I firmly believe that, if this were a true story, there would be no one left to write about it; the world would be taken out systematically by the undead, which Aspen Stationers' created when they released Lumiosa ink to the public.

It is my hope that readers are able to enjoy this book for what it truly is: A work of fiction that provides yet another take on zombies and how they might come to be walking, and terrorizing, among us. It is meant for entertainment, but I think the moral behind this made-up tale makes it possible to consider other possibilities, and hopefully, it causes readers to think about the items they are willingly choosing to consume.

LIVING LEGACY

ISBN-10: 0692517243 ISBN-13: 978-0692517246

Zombie Thriller

'Living Legacy: Among the Dead' is the first complete book I wrote. Though it is a very quick read, I believe readers will get just as much out of its pages as they would if it were a larger novel. Mostly, it was written for the sake of the love story which I have woven into the apocalyptic situation.

Alicia Gaden is a biology major at UCLA; she has her goals lined up and her future planned. She is also a very good student and person; she doesn't galivant around with different boys or party. Rather, she remains single, and keeps her primary focus on her studies.

Jace Booth is pretty much the same type of person as Alicia, with the exception being that he majors in chemistry. The pair meet up when everyone starts changing; people become violent, and their skin begins to pale and rot. For some reason, the two of them seem to have avoided drinking the water, allowing them to survive the strange phenomenon taking place, but together they pursue knowledge regarding why this is happening. As it turns out, there are no two better for the job.

The book is told from Alicia's perspective, which is not typical for me. I wanted to convey the zombie outbreak from the female point of view.

Alicia, in the initial pages, is pretty much on her own. Sure, she has a roommate, Lilith, but the girl really doesn't have much of a purpose, except for the sake of the reality of college life. No, Alicia is witnessing the changes in others entirely on her own. She wants to figure out what is happening and why it doesn't seem to be happening to her. She meets Jace during a trip to the UCLA student library, which turns out to be a relief because he seems unaffected as well.

Unbeknownst to the two of them, the problem is in the LA water supply. All-Purpose Plastics has been developing the 'plastic of the future': Soligel. Unfortunately, they push it through for federal approval, and an unaware maintenance man ends up disposing of a chemical spill improperly. He, too, is affected, but corporate executives take matters into their own hands and shut him up for good. It is only through their own tests and dangerous missions that Alicia and Jace are able to figure out that the problem is in the water. Once that is pinpointed, they must come up with a way to solve the outbreak before it is too late.

I wanted the main characters to be highly intelligent, but I also wanted them to be as courageous as possible. Let's face it, and I am sad to say, most college students today would panic and buckle if they found themselves in this situation. If these two are going to survive, and if any love is going to grow between them, it was essential for them to be strong and determined, and to have a mutually beneficial skill set if they wanted to get the job done. These are the main characteristics that were the foundation for Jace Booth and Alicia Gaden.

Now, it is true that I didn't really deal with the executives of All-Purpose Plastics in a manner that would be satisfying. The fact is, to me, they would be succumbing to the outbreak in their own time and manner. That would be their just deserts. In order for the book to have the combined flavors that I gave it, there was no room for justice, at least, not the kind of justice these people rightfully deserved. Greed and malice are sicknesses of the soul; it was best to let karma deal with them and focus on Alicia and Jace.

I added the tidbit regarding Alicia possibly becoming pregnant for a couple of different reasons. First, it would solidify their relationship and drive them on to continue the fight at hand at any cost. I wanted the relationship between the two of them to be held together by more than sex; my intent with these two was a lifelong commitment, even if there was the possibility that life could end at any second. Second, a pregnancy would be representative of life finding a way; this gives the reader a renewed sense of hope, both for the lives of the main characters, and for their success in completing their mission against the zombies and the tainted water.

I also wanted them to be able to conduct their research in a setting that provided them with some level of peace and comfort. This is where the house comes in. It was owned by a zombie victim named Belinda

Smythe, who is caught off guard by the undead monsters. Her car is left there, and has run itself out of gasoline. Finding this location was essential to their success; I mean, let's be real: If a couple of college kids are going to save the day and fall in love while they're at it, having a comfortable base of operations is essential.

Without giving away the ending, I would just like to say that Alicia and Jace are very crafty, and they have more than enough reasons to accomplish their goal to defeat the zombies and fix the issue successfully. But as we all know, a good story never ends without some kind of lure or suggestion about the real state of things. Perhaps Alicia and Jace firmly believe that they have fixed the problem in the water, but did they really? Only time will tell. I sincerely hope that readers enjoy 'Living Legacy: Among the Dead', and appreciate it for the fun piece of fiction it was meant to be.

ZOMBIE DIARIES

Homecoming Junior Year
ISBN-10: 0997876778 ISBN-13: 978-0997876772
Winter Formal Junior Year
ISBN-10: 0997876786 ISBN-13: 978-0997876789
Prom Junior Year
ISBN-10: 0997876794 ISBN-13: 978-0997876796

Girl Zombie

'Zombie Diaries" is a series I have written about the funny, off-beat story of Mavis Harvey, Girl Zombie. In the beginning of this first installment, the main character inadvertently drinks tainted tap water, and as the book progresses, she begins to experience some fairly crazy changes. As the introductory novel to the series, readers will get to know Mavis a bit, and they will get a strong sense of the personality of this girl who is slowly turning into a flesh-eating monster.

This is not a horror novel in the traditional sense, and I never intended it to be. What I wanted to do with Mavis and her life was have fun by asking, 'What would it be like if a normal, everyday girl were to experience this type of change alone, out of the blue? What if she retained her intelligence and logic, realizing something was happening, but not sure what? How would she deal with it?' I wanted the book to be light, with a tad of humor, and I wanted it to contain a story that was acceptable for reading for an audience of most any age.

In the beginning stages of Mavis' journey, she feels a little off but soon finds that her appetite has grown out of control overnight. She is a slight girl, so this gets the attention of her mother, who believes she is ill and takes Mavis to the doctor. Insisting that she feels great, and with no other real symptoms other than insatiable hunger, her physician diagnoses her with anemia, directs her to take iron supplements, and tells her mother to let her eat when she wants for the time being.

Unbeknownst to those in her life, Mavis soon begins to crave more than just an overabundance of food; she wants raw meat, and the bloodier the better. I used raw liver (of any kind) as her 'snack', so to speak, for a couple of different reasons. One: There really isn't a bloodier meat with a grosser texture; it seems to fit as a zombie snack perfectly, and two: Because most everyone hates liver, and the thought of it raw is unbearable. The temptation to gross out my readers was as irresistible to me as raw liver is to Mavis.

As her 'illness' slowly progresses, it begins to come out a bit in gray flaky spots on her skin and prominent dark veins showing through her flesh. She is getting pale, and her mother worries about that fact. Mavis also gains no weight, which is strange, because she is constantly eating one thing or another. Jane Harvey only mentions her concerns in passing, but when she catches her daughter eating a raw pork chop bone, she feels justified in her concerns. Mavis is a loving daughter and has always been trustworthy. Because she feels fine, she is able to tell her mother to not be worried, 'It's just the anemia'; Jane believes her.

I also felt that it was important to make Mavis very likeable; I wanted her to have strong morals and goals.

She is very friendly and kindhearted, but she doesn't hang around with a lot of friends. Indeed, she has only one, Kim Coleman, and they have been best friends since the first grade.

She likes boys, but has never been on a date simply because school has been more important, but also because she has never been asked. While she is pretty and slender, she also seemed a bit bookish and nerdy to the opposite sex; she knows it, and it never bothered her before. Kim is a bit heavy, very pretty, and just a tad self-absorbed; she has never dated either, possibly because of her friendship with Mavis.

After Mavis is 'infected', she is asked on her first date ever. A star football player for her high school tells her he has liked her for a long time, and works up the courage to ask her to the homecoming dance. At this point readers may begin to see Mavis as the teenager she is; as she begins to get to know love interest Jeff Deason, her feminine side begins to really show through her words and actions.

Mavis likes him very much, and she is excited about going to the dance with someone other than her best friend. The problem begins, however, when the pair start to date before the big event. She realizes that she can smell him, and he smells delicious, but so do a lot of other people.

With no real worries, she continues to get to know the young man and live her life, but when she dreams of eating a delivery man one day, she vows to never do such a horrible act. She is shocked and dismayed at her own dreams, but not because she killed a man; she is ashamed because she ate him, and that is the only reason. Convinced it is best to keep the dream to herself, Mavis continues with her plans for homecoming night with Jeff.

I didn't intend for ZD1 to be bloody, or scary. What my vision for Mavis consisted of was something laid-back and fun to read, something that takes an already insane idea (zombies) and turns it into a story that takes away the sting of the same old idea. With that in mind, readers of any age will enjoy the story of Mavis, and they will want to stick this crazy experience out with her until the bitter end.

I encourage you to enjoy 'Zombie Diaries' and continue to follow this tongue-in-cheek heroine as she slowly, but surely, comes to terms with what is happening to her.

OVERTAKEN CAPTIVE STATES

ISBN-13: 978-1948312004 ISBN-10: 194831200X
ISBN-13: 978-0692489314 ISBN-10: 0692489312
ISBN-13: 978-1948312127 ISBN-10: 1948312123

Supernatural Thriller

This particular novel was the second book that I have written, and it is the only one I have penned with a focus on alien invasion. I think that the premise of the book is good, and the story is fairly spooky overall.

The prologue consists of nothing but random characters in scattered cities. It relates the very first moments of the invasion of the Oppressors from varying points of view. As far as an introduction goes, it is superficial, but it is effective because of this fact. Once the invasion becomes confirmed reality, I introduce the main characters of the book and tell the story.

This is an invasion story that really doesn't have the obligatory 'happy ending'; nothing about this situation could possibly end happily for humans, and I wasn't going to pretend it could. But to me, the invasion itself is not the scariest part of 'Overtaken'; being tested to determine if you are of enough value to live or die is even more frightening. The pressure of the situation, and the truth that even if you pass the tests, you will go to a foreign planet forever, is a grim thing to have on one's shoulders. In the real world, people would commit suicide if faced with the prospect.

But there always has to be a hero or two, even if they ultimately are only saving themselves. The character of Josh Nichols takes readers to Washington, DC, with front row seats. Josh works as a code writer at the Pentagon. He is a young, ambitious man with all of his supposed ducks in a row. Something of a workaholic, Josh has no family or girlfriend in DC; he was born and raised in Iowa, so he's still fairly green behind the ears.

Kamryn Reynolds is Josh's polar opposite. With a history of crime and street-life, she is a seasoned, semi-tough computer hacker who is always dodging the law. When the invasion takes place, these two meet accidentally, and soon Josh is working side-by-side with her for the president himself. Together, they search for a weak spot in the computer system that is running all of the alien spacecrafts. Their plan is to hack into it and let down protective shields, making the Oppressors open to human attack.

In an effort to pick up the pace, I gave humankind a deadline, so to speak. In large numbers, people are led to testing facilities, separated from their families and never to be seen again. These groups are done by sections throughout each included city. Josh and Kamryn must get this all figured out before they are herded away for themselves.

What is the testing for? This was the fun part for me, because the concept does spark fear in my heart. So, am I being tested for strengths, or weaknesses? What will be done to me, extermination-wise, if I fail either way? Worse yet, what will happen to me if I 'pass'? It all consists of question marks which dance gleefully around the unknown, and the unknown is the scariest thing in the world.

Now, we should probably consider the question: With all of the resources and skills at the fingertips of the United States government, especially when it comes to employees, why choose Josh and Kamryn to try and save the day? Well, dear reader, I think the answer is obvious: It makes for a story that is much more fun and relatable. But seriously, isn't it hard to relate to every super-hero character there is? Real life consists of real people, and that's what these two kids represent.

'Superior' is another character I enjoyed playing with. He is the soulless, alien leader of the Oppressors, and his mission is destruction to his gain. He couldn't care less about these 'humans'. To him, they are like cockroaches in a deserted house; they must be exterminated before the new tenants can move in. From that perspective, it is his nature to be who he is and do what he is doing to humanity, just as it is our nature to love puppies and kitties and show compassion. The Oppressors are not able to think or feel in the same way.

The president, and all of his high-end, star-spangled advisors, are at a loss. The reason for this is simple: If aliens came, and they had the technology to get here, chances are they have it over on us. It would be a losing battle if indeed we had to fight one. None of their computer geniuses think like Kamryn or Josh, which forces the president's hand. I almost wrote these high-rankers as 'bumbling', because that's how I saw them in my mind's eye. They have been so busy thinking they were omnipotent that they never stopped to think about their own mortality. Bumbling, like I said.

Then we have the end. Yes, there are survivors; the Oppressors promised there would be. But there are more victims than escapees; the planet is virtually demolished. Not to mention the people who didn't pass and were killed, or worse yet, the ones stranded on the blazing, crumbling planet. I feel safe when I say there are no winners here, but there wouldn't be if this ever really happened, either.

I liked the way all of the 'hows' and 'whys' worked out the way they did. I hope readers have a good time with this grim story, and I hope that they get out of it all I put into it: From the fiction to the fear.

LUCIFER'S ANGEL

ISBN-10: 0692733280 ISBN-13: 978-0692733288

Supernatural Thriller

'Lucifer's Angel' is a book which tells the tale of a young girl raised in a very religious home, who experiences a year of terrible loss. The result of these painful occurrences is loss of the faith she has had her entire life, and in an effort to find a 'god' she can trust, the young teen turns to witchcraft. Unfortunately, she has no idea what she is getting herself into, and the consequences of her choice to revert are devastating.

Sarah Hathaway is your average teenager. She has lived in the fictional town of Paradise, her entire life, the only child of her parents, and their pride and joy. She has a very normal, happy life: Sarah has her best friend, Michelle, and her beloved border collie, Mitzi. She also has an uncommonly close relationship with her grandmother, church pianist Emma Holt. Everything in her life is perfect, and she is completely unprepared for the series of tragedies that take place.

For me, the best thing about writing 'Lucifer's Angel' was the freedom I had to add as many twists and surprises as I saw fit. This is an unpredictable book, and I like it that way. Even to the very last pages, when you finally think you have what is happening to Sarah figured out, I switch it up. But what I have to say is that the nature of this book is the perfect breeding ground for such surprise, and without it, this would not have come anywhere near making the point I intended it to make.

So, then, what is the point? Well, I could say there are a few, in fact. First, it is safe to say that we should never dabble in something we know nothing about. Hidden dangers lurk around every last corner in this world, and matters of spirituality are no exception. Whether you are a religious person or not, this is a fact, and Sarah learns this in a terrifying and painful way. Unfortunately for her, this lesson comes late.

Secondly, pain is a part of life. All of us go through doubt about our own beliefs and abilities. Sarah's doubt happens to run so deep, and her heart is so broken, that she makes the choice to turn to witchcraft almost strictly out of a sense of revenge toward God. 'If you won't give me my way, I'll find someone who will,' is essentially her thought process. Of course she is hurting, but we all do, and no one is exempt. When we turn our back on our own knowledge and beliefs because we are pouting over the facts of life, we sort of get what we deserve in the end. No amount of revenge or fit throwing will change the fact that bad things happen every single day.

I also try to convey the fact that it is terribly dangerous to give others too much trust. There are those in life that hold positions that should be trustworthy… pastors, parents, teachers, and the like. But we all know too well that everyone is human, and human beings are selfish by nature, not to mention capable of horrible things, no matter what their title or position is. This is especially true if there is something valuable to gain.

First, poor Sarah's grandmother passes while they are together. They are close, and this is the first death the girl ever experiences. She is torn apart, but after a bit, she tries to find her footing in life once again. Right after that, her dog is violently killed; since she is just getting over Grandma, this is like ripping a scab off a wound. Now it is a little harder for her to find her way back into the light. Suddenly, her lifelong best friend is moving two-thousand miles away… another great loss. The final straw is, her mother dies of cancer; all of these things happen in a very short period of time.

Besides her father, the only people she has for support are those from the church, and they are the last people she wants to talk to. Sarah begins to dabble in the craft, just studying and dabbling. After being bullied at school, resulting in personal injury, she decides to cast a spell on the culprit, and much to her great pleasure, it works. Next, she and new boyfriend Ryan Morris cast another, this time for money; this is just to confirm the power at their fingertips.

But things begin to take a scary turn. Ryan gets sick, and Sarah discovers someone evil is controlling the events in Sarah's life from the shadows, and the reason they are doing this is more devious and terrible than anyone can imagine. It takes the help of church member Laura McCain to educate Sarah and help her to confront the darkness which is threatening to consume her.

Yes, once again I have added surprises. Yes, I have twisted things in all the right places. But as I said above, this type of thing would be the nature of the black arts anyway; don't be surprised. The only thing I will admit to here is that I wish things could have gone differently for Sarah in her life; she is a likeable young lady who has promise. Unfortunately, her anger and decisions are her own worst enemy, and ultimately and sadly, this plays out in her life for you to read.

I hope you enjoy reading 'Lucifer's Angel', both for the joy of reading and for the points I have tried to make. It is a creative effort that consists of grief, horror, a bit of romance, and desperation. I have written about witchcraft before, but this story should drive things home and make them a bit more real.

STOLEN BLOOD

ISBN-10: 0997876743 ISBN-13: 978-0997876741

Vampire Thriller

'Stolen Blood' is the story of a secret society of vampires, all of whom live and work among us amicably, without murder or the intent to commit it. The difference between 'Stolen Blood' and other 'functional' vampire works which I have written is that these vampires are able to live the way they do through a pact with the 'Dark Father', to whom they offer a regular sacrifice in return for the ability to live off donated blood.

While I created several vampires who actively participate in this tale, the two main bloodsuckers are Mason Stout and Ira Stone. Mason has worked his way up to be the mayor of Philadelphia, Pennsylvania, while Ira Stone is the head of the massive conglomeration Stone and Kimble Pharmaceuticals. Stone also is the head of the secret society, and along with his wise assistant, is the only one permitted to seek out the will of the Dark Father in any given situation.

This society obtains their blood from a middleman by the name of Ross Berry. Berry is a gambling addict, something of a low-life, but he has the connections needed to obtain donated blood from a company called Bio-Donor, which he, in turn, sells at an atrocious price to the Society. But something happens along the line to Ross, disrupting this 'perfect' arrangement, and motivating Mayor Stout to seek out the assistance of another, Ross's friend and sidekick, Mike Biela. This is when the trouble begins.

The blood obtained by Mike is essentially 'bad', having undergone testing and other unknown 'treatment', which consists of genetic mutation. It is intended for the treatment of cancer, but Mike and those in the Society are unaware of this. Now, Mason Stout and those in his society 'sector' have consumed this blood, and it has reverted them back to the murderous state which they originally possessed. In a blood-induced 'high', Stout kills Mike Biela, and has to find the source of blood for himself, which he does, but only after killing a security guard and single father. Now, Stout must face the guard's grief-stricken and enraged daughter Sasha Hunter, who is being protected under the watchful eyes of Ira Stone; the leader knows that Stout must be stopped if the Society is to have any chance for redemption in the eyes of the Dark Father.

The first point I would like to make, which is vital to the story, is that while Mason Stout is the mayor of a major US city, he is also an egotist whose arrogant condition is aggravated by the bad blood. Sure, he is part of the Society, and he is being cared for by the Dark Father regardless of the negative state of his heart, but when his amplified condition puts all at risk, it is nothing to have to rid the earth of him.

Ira Stone is also a vampire, but his heart is in a much healthier state from the beginning. As the leader of the Society, it is his responsibility to make sure the others are cared for. Mason Stout manages to lose many who reside in his sector, and this fact alone is enough to make him a liability that needs to go. So, why is the help of the lamenting Sasha Hunter enlisted? Because she is obsessed as well as angry and because Ira is not able to do the deed himself; the elimination of Stout must be done by an outsider. Vigilante justice is the perfect solution.

Now, let's talk about the relationship between Ira and Sasha. Ira quickly gains her trust, almost stepping into the shoes of her deceased father immediately. Though she has no idea that the man is a vampire, she recognizes that he has the same intention as she: To rid the world of the murderous beast that killed her dad, though they both want this for differing reasons. Ira and Sasha quickly become fond of each other, and it takes little to no effort for her to trust this strange older man completely.

'Stolen Blood' is something of a far-fetched story that is heavy with originality and creativity. While it is a story about vampires, it is even more so a story about good versus evil, regardless of the fact that Ira Stone is at the helm when it comes to Mason's demise. It is important to understand that the Society, while made up of vampires, has crossed over into a new existence because of the Dark Father, which has pretty much rendered them 'good guys'.

As a heroine, Sasha Hunter is motivated by rage and deep grief. Anyone could have approached her with the killing of Stout and she would have jumped on the chance. To me, though, it was vital that the 'father figure' type do this, and as the compassionate and sensible leader of the Society, Stone was the ideal candidate to approach her, educate her, and train her, even though he had ulterior motives she has no idea about.

When I wrote this novel, I wanted to put a new skew on the whole vampire idea. This is not the first time I have done this, as long-time fans well know. Anyone familiar with my DeSai Trilogy is already aware that I enjoy creating vampires who live and walk among us, and 'Stolen Blood' is another of that sort.

This is a fun novel which definitely has its horrible moments. The concept is off-beat, but most readers enjoy a change as much as I revel in writing about one.

IN THE DEPTHS

(DeSai Trilogy Book 1)
ISBN-10: 0692721932 ISBN-13: 978-0692721933

Supernatural Thriller

This was the first installment of a vampire trilogy that I wrote involving a witch who is seeking immortality and all power by seducing the omnipotent head vampire of all time. It was also the first vampire book I wrote, and to be honest, one of the most detailed and fun books I have written. I believe that this ongoing saga is deep, engaging, and entertaining.

Cyril DeSai is a centuries-old vampire who has been wreaking havoc and causing terror in the hearts of men the world over. There is more to his behavior than simply murderous feeding; Cyril wants a family of his own that he can lord over and 'love'. In order for that to properly happen, he needs a queen, and finding the right woman is at the heart of his quest. Unfortunately, not just anyone will do; most women give in to his every desire, and he needs one who is capable of taking care of the 'family' in his unforeseen absence, one who will keep his dream alive.

'In the Depths' is written in a manner which allows the fictional vampire characters to live and walk among us. Once DeSai gets the ball rolling by attacking a SCUBA diver in the depths of a cave in Honduras, it is just a matter of time before his kind slowly begins to take over, and this will bring him to full power, in accordance with his plan. The Earth, ultimately, will belong to him, and it will exist only under his rule or the rule of his queen, once she is found. I enjoyed toying with this idea; the thought of all of us wandering around, living our day to day lives without suspicion is basically what we all do every day. Having vampires run the show is pretty much representative of the governments that rule over us. This is one thing that differs in this vampire story when it is compared to others.

Another point that differs and takes this story on its own unique path is the concept of a witch 'mating' with a vampire, and even being bitten for the sole purpose of enjoying life eternal. She is already evil to the core, with her own selfish motives lying at the root of every decision she makes. The outcome, while initially unknown, is the basis for the other two installments in this trilogy, and there are some interesting ideas I added here and there in regards to what would happen if such a union were to take place, even in the fictional realm.

So, with Cyril DeSai seeking all power, Rasia Engres enters the picture. Rasia comes from a long line of witches, and while most of them were 'good' witches (or at least, behaved in a socially acceptable manner), Rasia is rotten through and through. She has basically hated men and their incessant sexual advances for her entire life, so seeking out a true vampire and usurping his plans means nothing to her.

Rasia is strikingly beautiful, with long, lush red hair and emerald eyes. She is slender and toned, and extremely confident in all of her ways. Now, DeSai has always been able to have any woman he wants; he is extremely attractive himself, and his hypnotic manner and ability turn each of them into putty in his hands. Typically, he tires of them quickly, but Rasia is a different story. The beautiful journalist sweeps him off his feet with little effort, and it doesn't take long for the bird to become the prey.

While DeSai is nothing more than a black-hearted spawn of Satan, I wanted him to be somewhat likeable for the reader. I wanted him to be loaded with such sex appeal and confidence that even his most morbid behaviors became easy to overlook. In the first pages, this was a bit difficult, because realistically, Cyril DeSai is a murderous vampire. But once Rasia comes onto the scene, this daunting task lightened a bit. The 'victor' is to become the victim; now the reader is able to sympathize with him on a different level, which honestly sets the tone for both of the next two books.

Is this trilogy far-fetched? Of course! It's a vampire witch story! But it is highly enjoyable directly due to its unbelievability. The point here is not 'Could this really happen'. The point is: what would happen if a witch was able to secure a vampire bite successfully? And what if she was a bad witch by nature? And worse yet, what if she became the head of the most powerful country in the world?

It is also important to point out that, while the people of Earth are all being changed into vampires, those who haven't yet been changed have no idea about the monsters they are surrounded by, and this is part of the big plan. It is an easy takeover for DeSai, a takeover which is based almost slowly on his ability to sweet talk, manipulate and lie. So, is his destiny with Rasia deserved? Almost absolutely! Even after readers learn who he was in the past, before his 'fall' to evil, after they learn of his children and wife, and the way he became who he is, it is impossible to ignore the fact that he is now, a killer. Sympathy may go out the window, but I intended to recreate any feelings of pity one may have for DeSai when I wrote the two follow-up books; I believe I accomplished that goal, as readers will discover when they continue with two and three.

I was highly entertained with the smug, selfish nature of the characters, and it was a joy to bring them to life as I did. I only hope readers enjoy them as much as I did writing them.

WITCHES IMMORTAL

(DeSai Trilogy Book 2)
ISBN-10: 0692722165 ISBN-13: 978-0692722169

Supernatural Thriller

'Witches Immortal' is the second installment in my DeSai Trilogy. Essentially, this series is a vampire tale, but in this, book two, the main character, Rasia Engres, is also a witch. The entire point, besides being an entertaining work of fiction, is to find out about the woman who killed DeSai in book one on a much more personal level.

Rasia is a witch through and through, and she really doesn't have an ounce of love in her soul. This is something I wanted to make clear in 'In the Depths', but even more so here. The most effective way to do that, in my opinion, was to let the readers really get to know her and have an understanding of the reality that a number of circumstances made her who she is. Excuses aside, the woman is evil to the core, and she is truly the perfect mother for the child she is carrying.

So, as readers get to know Rasia, they will also get the scoop on Cyril DeSai from a differing perspective of that given in the first book. Now things are all about the woman who took his life: how she came to know who and what he was, and how she pretty much put herself in a position to take things over. She is crafty and conniving, and she won't think twice about causing pain to another for whatever reason.

Rasia Engres is also a very beautiful woman; her high intelligence level is simply the icing on the cake. She is a tall, slender woman with red hair and green eyes, and her taste in clothing is impeccable. Being a professional woman who is actively climbing the ladder of success, she is able to impose her stern personality often, especially with co-workers and underlings.

Intimate relationships don't really interest her; in fact, she was a virgin when she gave herself to DeSai. Rasia has other things on her mind in life, and they have nothing to do with lying around and making love. She has also been put in very uncomfortable positions by men in her life, as you will read, and this had stirred up a fair amount of rage toward the opposite sex. This point contributes greatly to her virginity being intact for so long in her life.

Rasia can be driven to do 'good', if I could call it that, but only if there is something in it for her. Take, for instance, the serial murderer who is stalking the women of Kiev. Rasia, being a top journalist for the Kiev Post, decides to pursue the killer on her own, and reap the benefits of his sacrifice. For one thing, she is disgusted with what he is doing to women, and she believes he needs to die. But on the other hand, she'll get off killing the murderer anyway, so it's a no-brainer for her to chase him down. Her entire way of thinking is skewed, and any good she does is just the inevitable part of a sick ripple effect.

Now, back to the 'witch' aspect of things. Rasia is not just a witch by practice alone, she is a witch by blood. The line goes back for generations, and let me tell you, these are some husband-killing, child-sacrificing witches. She has been taught by the writings of her Grandmother Anfisa in the sacred Book that if a witch were to sustain a vampire bite, she would not only live eternally, but she would have power unsurpassed, as well. This is the driving force behind everything Rasia Engres does in her life, from her career choice to every last sacrifice; if there is a true vampire walking the earth, Rasia intends to find him.

Once she finds him, however, he must bite her, and she is pretty sure that it isn't easy to dictate who a vampire will bite. The good news is she is stunningly beautiful, she is accomplished, and as a witch, she is somewhat resistant to DeSai's more hypnotic qualities. Rasia is a confident woman with a strong mindset: Come hell or high water, she will get her bite.

She doesn't sound like someone who would have enough nurturing ability in her little finger to birth and raise a child, but by the end of the book, it is obvious that is exactly what she is going to do. It is here that I realized it was important to soften her up a bit, no matter how little. Yes, she is going to have a baby, but she is still a terrible person; I felt the best approach was for her to begin to rue the killing of Cyril, and maybe she realizes that she loved him just a bit. This is a burden that Rasia Engres must bear for her own eternity.

'In the Depths' and 'Witches Immortal' are basically the story of a vampire and a witch who make a baby; the trilogy will culminate with his birth and life in book three. Cyril DeSai was a manipulative vampire who actually began to take over the world. Rasia Engres is the beautiful witch who rips it all from his hands. Their child will put them both to shame. When discussing only Rasia, however, she can stand on her own two feet in any situation, with no exception. While I despised her as a person, I loved her as a character, and she was actually one of my favorites to write about. She will continue on in book three, and fans will get to see how life, and its random series of events, brings everyone to their knees, including vampires and witches.

I had fun writing 'Witches Immortal', and I hope you get just as much enjoyment out of it when you read it. I found it entertaining to develop the character of Rasia, taking over with her from 'In the Depths', and I don't believe you will be disappointed. The woman certainly is evil through and through.

LUCIEN'S REIGN

(DeSai Trilogy Book 3)
ISBN-10: 069272219X ISBN-13: 978-0692722190

Supernatural Thriller

The third and final book in my DeSai Trilogy is entitled 'Lucien's Reign', and it tells the story of the culmination of Cyril DeSai and Rasia Engres in their son, Lucien. Ultimately, Lucien's existence has been the key all along; his mother Rasia and even his father Cyril were only mere pawns in the game the Powers are playing. This final installment chronicles his life until he finally comes into complete power at the age of eighteen.

At the very beginning of the book, Rasia is in the throes of labor. Now, to readers who are familiar with her character from reading the first two, she is a hard, dark woman with nothing but evil intent in her heart. She has murdered the vampire Cyril DeSai, but not until after they have made passionate love. Pregnant with his child, she picked up his mantle and continued on as his wife and head of the new DeSai family, which he has been creating.

Rasia is aware that her son is something of a 'chosen' one. He has a purpose set firmly in stone by the Powers, and the fact that he is the most horrific of breeds, a cross between a vampire and a witch, makes him dangerous from the beginning. At times, you may notice that she is apprehensive when it comes to him, almost as if she is afraid of him. Because she is so hateful, it is a bit satisfying, in a sense, for her to be fearful of another, particularly her own child.

Her trepidation turns out to be justified: Lucien is the son of Satan himself; not a man, but an animal with insatiable appetites that he cannot even begin to comprehend. So basic are these instincts, and so powerful, that Lucien doesn't even give them a second's consideration. He simply does what feels good and what pleases him at the moment.

The birth of Lucien Cerebus DeSai is nothing but a threat to Rasia, and this interferes with her affection. She is afraid of the Powers, as she should be, so she confirms. Otherwise, as far as her son goes, he is nothing more than the one who would take the rule from her hands; she would eventually be his slave. She hates him, deep inside; there is really not an ounce of true affection in her soul for the boy she carries and births.

I wanted a certain level of normalcy and balance to remain in the world in this book, even though the majority of the population are vampires. The only way to accomplish this was through the mean-spirited Rasia; I had to play up her mothering instincts, and I had to make Cyril's family dream become her dream as well. Only in this way would she raise Lucien with the iron fist necessary for him to become an effective family head. All character defects aside, she does the best she can; she schools him herself and basically keeps him isolated, with the exception of a single female friend, who eventually becomes his betrothed.

Isabella Scarlet Gilliam is the daughter of Patrick, the first bitten by DeSai while on a scuba diving trip when DeSai began to build his family. She is the voice of reason and the rock of stability throughout Lucien's life; she knows him like no other, bearing witness to, and keeping all of his secrets. She adores him as the night adores the moon, and she looks forward to the day she will be his wife. She, like Lucien, is a 'half-breed'. Her mother is human a majority of Isabella's life. Lucien is unaware of his witch vampire lineage until later in the book, as you will see.

Isabella also suffers an abundance of heartache and grief when it comes to her love. At one point, Lucien goes through a sort of 'vampire puberty' that sends him off on insane sexual tangents. For a long period, he completely puts Isabella out of his life, and she attempts to go on with her own, her love continuing to burn. But her own mother Rose will not allow her to have a relationship with another because Isabella's marriage to Lucien is inevitable; it is the will of the Powers. The girl must bear her burdens alone.

I should also mention the other signs of wickedness that Lucien displays in his life, though more often than not, are only visible to you, the reader. Rasia knows he is sick, but she is unaware of all he really does; he is deceitful and conniving like no other child before him, and he hides his fun and games well. Rasia finds herself on her knees before the powers, even asking to end her own son's life, to no avail. The Powers demand that she fulfill her given task: To raise the boy to maturity and power.

Writing 'Lucien's Reign' was a good time; I was able to really cut loose in a lot of areas regarding the true enormity of Lucien's evil character while attempting to help readers embrace any iota of humanity that he may possess. I believe I also dealt justice wisely to Rasia for all of her sins, and I think that the reader will agree. For those who have read this book, or the entire series, I do hope you had as much fun with these sick characters as I have.

ABOUT THE AUTHOR

I am a father of two beautiful children, Jon and Kim. They are my motivating forces; they are the lighthouse in this vast ocean. In this life, they are the air that I breathe; they are the oasis in this desert of uncertainty. They are my greatest joy in life, and my number one priority. I have a long list of hobbies, and I attribute that to my lust for life! I like to surround myself with positive people, who share the same interests. Family values, the arts, outdoors, nature, and travel are tops on my list. I embrace attending cultural and artistic events because I believe dramatic self-expression is the window to the soul. I wear my heart on my sleeve, and I still believe in chivalry, and I always treat people the way I want to be treated.

www.rwkclark.com

85607469R00176

Made in the USA
Lexington, KY
03 April 2018